# *Book of Never*

Blood of the Guardian

Ashley Capes

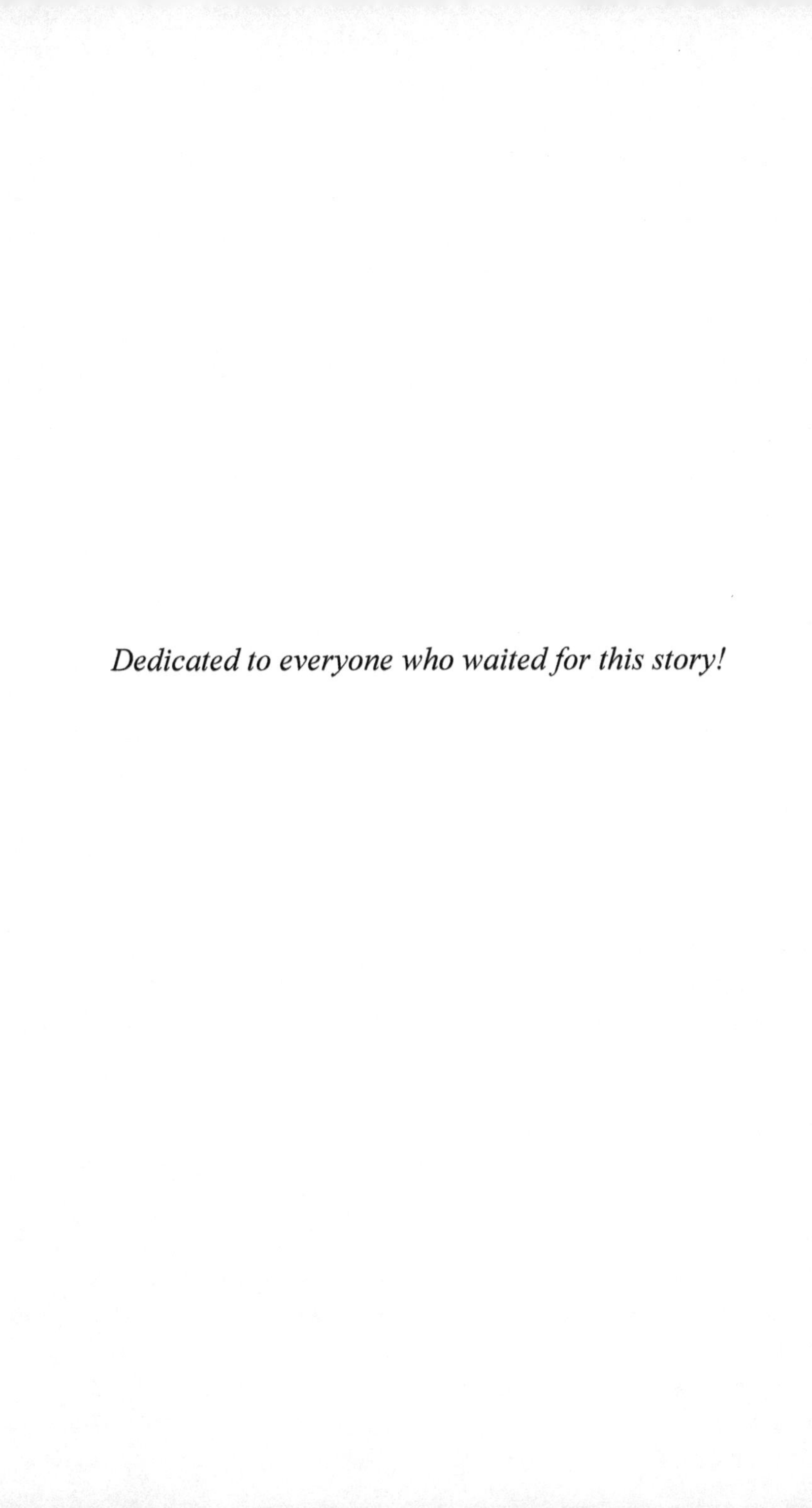

*Dedicated to everyone who waited for this story!*

# Prologue

Autumn

"The mongrel that refers to himself as 'Never' will approach the Seat of Facets."

Never glared up toward the disembodied voice where it spoke from somewhere within the shadowy hall – a fine contrast, considering all of the white elsewhere. Chains clinked as he shuffled forward. Blood trickled across his skin from barely-healed wounds that covered his half-naked body.

Wounds that refused to heal.

Old wounds, reopened.

The glare was all he could manage in the way of defiance, considering the gag of lilac-soaked cloth that stung his tongue and seared his airways. Not to mention the lilac ropes that bound him.

The Conclave sat arranged in such a way that their faces and robed-torsos remained in shadow, with only hands resting upon their knees visible – and even those very hands seemed covered by the robes.

The voice, the owner of which remained hidden, continued to speak for the Conclave.

"Offer both Apologies and Regret. Do so, and you may be permitted to select the form of your execution."

# Chapter 1.

Summer

Amouni flew overhead, their wings bright against a sky of stretching blue.

Piercing sunlight warmed Never's upturned face, a sharp contrast to the cool, glittering lake where he and Rikeva were treading water. Not that he moved with any rigour, considering where he found himself.

Considering that they were now trapped in the ancient past…

The time of the Amouni.

So far, in a probable blessing, they had not drawn anyone's attention. Not even from the not-too distant dolphin-shaped boat and its passengers; mostly robed Amouni who smiled and laughed – a carefree sound. Thankfully, they appeared focused only on their drinks or each other.

In contrast, paler Hanik who waited upon them – if that's who the servants were – did not appear cheerful at all.

Rikeva nudged him, her eyes wide. "There's so many."

He nodded. Tension and doubt were already chipping away at his awe. Had the Eye of Hours actually completed its work? How? It had been destroyed! Yet denying the evidence before him was futile… He turned back toward the shore. There, a tree-lined walkway skirted the lake, pink and red shrubs catching the eye. Beyond, darker shapes of the mountains.

Utterly inconclusive.

Something caught his leg.

It yanked down, shadows covering him and cutting Rikeva's cry short.

Coloured lights of rose and white streaked all around, blinking within a dry darkness. Yet it did not last. He soon found himself standing in a familiar vestibule, not a drop of water falling from his clothing or hair. A Guide waited nearby. The thing's animal-head was something grey, with wrinkled skin and large ears – and white fangs that protruded from an empty mouth. Unlike some Guides Never was familiar with, every part of this one remained bright and clear, with no hints of anything missing or decaying.

*The Vestibule is attended.* As ever, it bore a flat voice. *Are you unwell, Master?*

"No." At least, not in the way the Guide seemed to be asking. "Why?"

*We have various Alleviators at the Temple Trivium, should you require their services. However, the same is not permitted for your guest.*

"No?"

*The Untamed do not share the same rights as Subjects of the Fountain.*

He narrowed his eyes, but not at the unfamiliar description of the Amouni people. "Do not refer to her that way."

*Yes, Master.*

Rikeva had folded her own arms, displeasure clear. By whatever magic, she obviously understood the Guide, who had spoken in Amouni. Perhaps a feature to assist visitors to the temple?

"I trust there will be no objections if we both enter," he asked.

*None at all. All are welcome to pay their respects.*

Never waited.

The Guide did not answer, nor did it move to open the door – for now, concealed within the patterned tiles.

"Are you taking us?"

*When entering via the Vestibule, your blood is required, Master.*

Never drew a knife and pricked his forefinger. Red bloomed, and he placed it upon the thin podium.

Light pulsed… and then nothing.

The Guide blinked. *Master, please wait.*

"Is something wrong?" Never managed to keep his voice even. Despite the fact that the Guide would not harm him, that it recognised him as one of its masters, it had clearly been created to consider Rikeva as lesser – an unacceptable risk.

*I have sent for a Guardian.*

He tensed. "Why?"

"That doesn't sound good, Never," Rika said.

"Agreed. Whatever it is, I'll be able to convince them. Best we don't antagonise anyone, even the Guides."

"Right."

A robed figure appeared with barely a glimmer of light. She was armed with a belt knife only but unlike the Guide, she was human. Even so, she did not greet them. Instead, the woman frowned at the podium bearing Never's blood. Her long, dark hair seemed to move almost independently to the rest of her as she examined it.

He cleared his throat. "Hello?"

When she finally glanced up at Never, not even seeming to register Rikeva, the Guardian's blue eyes were not welcoming. "You are a mongrel."

# Chapter 2.

The Guardian had escorted them through dim tunnels and into a room Never had not seen anywhere in the Temple Trivium when facing the Burnished King. Of course, Oleksan had not been offering tours.

How different would the place appear anyway, being so many years in the past?

One thing was clear; they were still deep beneath the temple.

Smooth walls appeared to be steel of pure white – not tiles as he was expecting – with occasional lines of luminous blue quartz running throughout. Some of it even looked organic; they may well have represented veins, based on their somewhat meandering paths.

The blue did not streak through any of the clear quartz that divided the room into three chambers. In each section rested a silver chair, exactly the same as the one to which Never found himself strapped. Bound by soft rope with a lilac scent, Never somehow understood, without even attempting escape, that it would prevent him from using his fire.

Even if he could access his Amouni gifts, they would not get him far.

Like Rikeva in the next section, he was very much a prisoner. A pair of Amouni in white robes and black masks that had been shaped into eagle-beaks, examined her, their movements gentle. She did not seem under immediate threat – none of the silver tools that waited on small, wheeled stands were being used.

Yet.

*Not even on me.*

So far, his own pair of Amouni attendants did not seem willing to remain very close, asking their questions from a few steps away. Had they come to loom over him, attack would still have been difficult – not even the eyeholes of their masks offered a weak spot, since those, too, were filled with clear quartz.

Above all, it was the Guardian who posed the greatest threat to escape.

She continued to regard him with deep concern from her position in the far corner of the room.

"We've been here for some time," Never said. "You could introduce yourself. Or tell me a story. You must have a favourite food? At this point, I'd even settle for another question."

Nothing.

"Or better than any of that, I'd accept your apology after you free us."

"Min is my name." She began to count off items with her fingers. "You are not catalogued. Your accent is not registered either. Your claims of being from distant lands are vague and unsatisfactory." She stopped to lift a small sphere of quartz where a single drop of his blood floated within. The droplet was restless as it searched its confinement, becoming wild tendrils as he watched. "And above all, you carry the filthiest blood I have ever encountered – by many magnitudes, worse than even the Strays."

He raised an eyebrow. "What a charming description."

"An *accurate* description." She placed the sphere into her robe-pocket and folded her arms. "All the lesser peoples can be found within your blood, including a vast amount with grand delusions or faulty memories – many deeply fragmented. The same can even be said for the Amouni we have found. Two Guardians at least, and they also carry faulty memories. Not only that, but there are beasts here too!"

Never nodded.

"Further, they are not limited to common ones, stranger. But Distinguished Creatures in addition to pure abominations. Traces of the Malecaphera, traces of a twisted thing that should not exist, along with things we cannot yet recognise."

"Don't forget the Phoenix," he said.

She narrowed her eyes. "No, I am not forgetting the Great Phoenix."

"And?"

"There's a chance you have somehow managed to… fake all of this."

He chuckled. "Is that what you believe?"

The Guardian approached, and a hint of exasperation entered her tone – perhaps at the failure to solve the riddle before her. "No. I do not understand how this is so, but I cannot believe you could have harmonised that which passes for the blood in your veins. And so I will ask you once more. Who are you? From where do you hail? And what is your purpose at the Temple?"

It was probably time to see if she was actually willing to negotiate or whether she planned to keep him prisoner forever. "Give me assurances."

"Being?"

He glanced through the quartz divider to where Rikeva seemed to be repeating herself – even with whatever the Amouni were using to help with communication, they were obviously having trouble understanding her. And why not? It was probably quite difficult to translate language from a future that had not yet come to pass. "No-one harms her. Not a single hair upon her head."

"To do such is not our way."

Difficult to believe her response for many reasons. Especially considering a reception that was both hostile *and* somewhat detached. As though the Amouni were examining unclean things that still had the potential to be quite useful. "It most assuredly *is* the Amouni way, so I would have you swear an Oath as Guardian."

Guardian Min's jaw fell open and her two attendants turned, as if to gauge her reaction.

"I see you don't like your honour being challenged," Never said.

"No, I do not."

He shrugged. "Then imagine being called a 'mongrel' full of filthy blood, and being imprisoned, interrogated and examined, instead of helped."

"But you are definitely a mongrel."

Never snorted then – she really was sticking to her

conclusion. "I admire your stubbornness. So, is that your answer?"

"No. Are you offering full cooperation?"

"I am." And finally, there was a little more help from Ecanseja's memories. For if the Guardian agreed, she was binding not only herself but those of her station generally and, specifically, those working under her care.

Although 'supervision' was more likely.

It would not be a literal binding, but certainly Amouni obsession with status meant she could not afford to bring the Guardians as a whole into disrepute. More, she had to not only act in a way considered more honourable than the 'lesser people', but also to be *seen* doing so.

Above all, she would personally suffer a loss in standing and position herself if she became directly or indirectly responsible for harm coming to Rika.

If the Amouni agreed.

"Then I will swear as you request. My Oath I offer to you: from Sacred Blood to Sacred Blood, I will protect the stranger known as Rikeva of Marlosi." She leant in, close enough that he could now see flecks of gold throughout the blue of her eyes. "There. The whole truth this time. Please, stranger."

He nodded. "You might want a chair of your own."

# Chapter 3.

Guardian Min had moved both him and Rikeva to a new room, then promptly disappeared with assurances that she'd return quickly. Little in her expression had revealed precisely what she thought of his story; and while he'd held back plenty of personal history, the struggle over the Eye of Hours was given in detail.

At least, without mentioning much about Snow or Ecanseja.

He might not be able to keep all his secrets forever. Especially depending on the time it took the Amouni to decipher the memories within his blood. Still, it was better to keep them in the dark as long as possible.

Their new quarters were not exactly guest rooms of the Temple, and once again, a place unfamiliar from his last visit. Similar white walls but no thin, blue glow. Instead, a single painting covered almost an entire wall – a seascape full of fanciful ships; a regatta, rather than a battle.

"Never, this isn't much of a plan," Rikeva said. "They're not going to believe us. Or her, despite that oath."

He turned from the painting. "Probably not. But I'm still thinking."

"Got anything?"

"No. You?"

"Nothing," she said with a shake of her head. "I can't stop thinking about this whole thing. Why are we here? In the past?"

"Something went wrong when Cog destroyed the Eye of Hours – just not in the way we'd hoped."

"Right. And wasn't the Eye supposed to change everything on a *far* larger scale?" She strode to his side. "Even with the size of that crystal or the Burnished King's power, is this really possible?" Traces of shock lingered in her eyes. "Even standing here now, seeing all the Amouni, I don't know if it's real."

He took her hands. "I know."

"Never, say something better."

"I'd love to," he replied with a grin. "But I think we have to accept that even if we were free to swim across the lake, the land we'd find on the other side would be that of the ancient past, yes. That was Oleksan's plan."

Her grip tightened. "Then what about everyone else? Are they gone now? Everyone and everything we know, gone? Or was it just the two of us somehow tossed back here when we touched the crystal?"

"The latter. I hope."

She sighed. "Well… we're at the mercy of the Amouni now. Do you think we can trust them?"

"No." There was no need to hesitate. "Once we know what they want, we use that to find a way home. Or at the very least, escape."

"You're making it sound easy."

"Easy would be nice for once," he said with another grin. "What about you? They didn't hurt you, did they?"

"No. It was only questions about my bloodline. And my Weaving," she said. "They recognise it, but I don't think they understood."

"The barrier of language?"

"At first. But somehow, they found a way to teach me Amouni. I can speak and understand it well enough," she said, switching to the dead tongue.

Before Never could ask more, the door opened with a soft click.

It revealed Guardian Min and a young Amouni man with a bald head and the symbol of a wand upon his grey robe. The wand featured a half-circle about two-thirds of the way to the top. His eyes were awfully bright and he seemed to be fighting off a smile.

"Welcome to the Temple Trivium." His voice was deep, and he licked his lips before continuing. "I am Jeymiyu."

"You seem a little too-pleased to see us, Jeymiyu," Never said.

"I do apologise for my excitement. Your story is remarkable and has caught my interest. But if you would allow me a final test, I believe you and your companion will be escorted to the nearest palace as honoured guests."

Never raised an eyebrow. "Even a mongrel can be an honoured guest?"

"Most certainly."

Doubtful. "And are you a Guardian, like Min here?"

"No, I am only a Supreme."

Guardian Min inclined her head as she took a seat nearby.

"You flatter me, Supreme Jeymiyu."

The man waved away her words.

"Supreme is a modest title," Never observed. "Born or earned?"

The Guardian's mouth fell open, but Jeymiyu only smiled. "Born, but I know my worth. More importantly, that was a sincere question, wasn't it?"

"Of course."

"Hmm… You are either a fine liar or you truly *have* arrived from a future barren of the Chosen." He looked to the Guardian. "He may not possess knowledge of Amouni custom, propriety or hierarchy, at all."

"At this point, we cannot know for certain either way," Guardian Min said.

"Verily."

Never shrugged. "Then what good will your final test be?"

"I won't know that until I complete it," the so-called Supreme said. "A mere moment." He stepped closer and gazed into Never's eyes. True to his word, the test was swift indeed, as the man was soon stepping back to call for a Guide.

Another figure with the head of the strange, grey animal slipped into view. *Master?*

"Please ensure the Air Rail is prepared – one with seating for four."

*Immediately, Master.*

"Follow us, please," the Supreme said, and took them into another pale hall and through an intersection of passages, stopping at a tall, quartz window. He pressed the quartz and it slid open.

The young man stepped within and gestured for them to follow, room enough easily for four.

And then it was rising.

Never reached for a handhold as did Rikeva, but the passage was smooth. Like the steel box found in the Amber Isle? Significantly more sophisticated, however.

Their ascent ended at a platform open to the elements, perhaps halfway up the Temple. It revealed a grand view of the sparkling lakes below, and one of the other towers – distant, but not so far that he couldn't see winged Amouni landing.

"How does it stay in place?" Rikeva asked.

Never finally noticed that she was asking after the Air Rail. Yet the name was misleading, since it offered no rail at all. It was merely a floating carriage of white, as best he could discern.

Hanging above the lake and its boats far, far below. Ornate handles and carvings aplenty covered the sleek carriage, where a small but bright-blue glow escaped from the underside.

"Magic, I suppose, would be the simplest answer," the Supreme told Rikeva. "It is one of the Temple's most recent marvels – all the palaces are rushing to duplicate our work, which gives me great satisfaction. Please enter, it is safe."

She did so with a frown, Never close behind.

Their escorts sat across from them – he with a smile, and she with a more neutral expression by far. A hint of fear? Unlikely, if she bore wings, as likely for a Guardian.

"Is there a *forasa* symbol upon the Temple's top?" Never asked.

"Yes. Though we may have to convince the Forasa

Guardians to allow your companion to use it, as the Untamed are generally not –"

The steel tip of Rikeva's staff was suddenly *quite* close to his crotch. "You must know some other words," she said.

She'd spoken Quisoan, but whether either Amouni understood her words or not, they still exchanged a glance of doubt, since the staff conveyed its own direct message.

Supreme Jeymiyu spoke first. "Of course."

Never leant forward. "Whatever your true purpose with us may be, you are not convincing me that we are honoured guests."

Guardian Min's expression dropped into a frown. "We are showing great restraint at such uncivilised behaviour."

He frowned. "Oh, so am I."

Doubt flickered across her eyes. For all her examination of his blood, she wasn't certain what he was capable of. A fact he would have to exploit.

But Supreme Jeymiyu offered another ingratiating smile, hands raised. "You are absolutely guests. The Fountain will be delighted to meet you both. After all, you could change the entire world. You are vital. Both of you," he added, with a glance at Rikeva. Only, the enthusiasm did not reach his eyes.

Rikeva lowered her weapon. "I see."

"Why is that so?" Never asked. The Fountain, whatever it might have been, was obviously important to Amouni hierarchy, but Ecanseja's memories were not speaking.

"I could not estimate exactly. Yet from what Guardian Min has told me, even if your claim about the future is not true, we believe your blood is of great interest. With so much unknown, it could improve the lives of many, many peoples."

"Then, do they suffer under Amouni governance?" Never asked.

"Oh, I don't believe so. Our guidance is most assuredly of benefit to all."

The Guardian frowned. "This conversation does not strike me as cooperative on your part, Never."

"Once you stop insulting Rikeva, and once you explain exactly what my blood will be used for, and then once you explain when we will be permitted to continue on our way – I assure you, I will become more agreeable."

"Many of those questions are best left to the Conclave, or the Fountain."

"Onward, then."

# Chapter 4.

Never stepped from the Air Rail's carriage onto the roof of the central tower then onto intricately paved stone, each piece white save for a trail of rose quartz. It led to the *forasa*, where their escorts had moved to speak with a pair of Guides… who were quite familiar.

Silver robes left their muscled arms bare and both wore identical human faces – grey hair and clean-shaven cheeks with dark beards… Exactly like the guards he and Snow fought on the Stair of Winds.

"Never."

Rikeva drew him toward a ledge and its broad stairwell, leaving the others out of earshot. When she stopped, it offered another impressive view of the sparkling Evache Lakes, rolling green plains and mountains beyond. The second, bright tower waited to his left, with more Amouni flying from various directions.

Exactly how many Amouni were Ascended?

Detail upon those that approached to pass between the numbered arches below was easier to make out. They bore wings of varying shades – mostly from white to black, but also grey and purple, and sometimes even a pale yellow.

Clothing was less varied, being mostly robes of silver or muted colours. Sometimes, the Amouni wore tunic and pants that left their arms bare, as if fashioned after the Guides. Or, more likely of course, the Guides were fashioned after their masters.

"Are you sure about this?" Rikeva asked. "We don't actually know where we're going. Or who or what this Fountain is."

"I know." He gestured to the sky. "But if we tried to fly away, we wouldn't be faster than the slowest Amouni."

She glowered back at their escorts. "I don't trust either of them."

"Neither do I."

"Then I have an idea." She lowered her voice, stepping closer, enough that the freckles across the bridge of her nose were clear as she switched to Quisoan. "Can you have the *forasa* send us somewhere else?"

"I don't know." It was a wonderful idea, and absolutely worth attempting.

"We can land somewhere distant and give ourselves a moment to plan something. Such as who might be able to help us."

"Someone like the Great Phoenix of Kiymako?"

She nodded. "If no-one else, surely the Phoenix."

Footsteps approached. Guardian Min stopped, her arms folded. A rising breeze pulled at her hair, strands passing over her eyes. It did not change her gaze, however. That remained stern.

"Is the Supreme having trouble?" Never asked her.

"Nothing that will not be resolved shortly."

"What do you want to ask?" Rikeva held her staff in such a way that suggested she was ready to use it, without actually taking an attacking stance.

"Nothing. I have come to give Never some advice."

"I can guess. You want me to be mindful of my manners when we meet the Fountain."

She frowned. "For your own good. The Fountain – or the Conclave – will decide your fate. And hers, if that matters to you."

The Guardian had a point, of course. And while Ecanseja's knowledge of the Fountain was now within reach of his fingertips – fingertips of his mind, at least – Never didn't reveal what little he knew. Instead, it would be more valuable to see what she offered, and what she held back.

For the Fountain was not so much a fount as a... sapping figure.

An entity that seemed part oracle and part devourer. And more. But what exactly, Ecanseja may not have known. Few met the Fountain directly, even amongst Guardians and Supremes or Ascended.

"Is there something else we should know about the Fountain?"

"That its hunger is unfathomable," she replied. "Which might work in your favour. But the Conclave will be the first hurdle. They will judge your suitability to even be presented to the Fountain. Despite Supreme Jeymiyu's enthusiasm, the Conclave may not approve."

"So be it. If that is what they decide, we will be on our way."

"If the Conclave do not reach agreement, you will both

likely be executed, though for differing reasons. You must convince them you are of value, in some way."

Finally, some welcome advice, if not welcome news. "How difficult will they be to convince?"

"Perhaps easily."

"Perhaps?"

"I cannot predict. But if you have not lied, if you have not harmonised falsities within your own blood, then perhaps. It *would* explain your discomfort when we discuss the… non-Amouni peoples."

"You mean when you denigrate them. But please, continue."

She glared at him. "I am trying to help you."

"And how does your implication that I am a liar do that?"

"I am trying to explain that if the words we have used today are a problem, then you will find the Conclave utterly obsessed with purity," she snapped.

"Join us," Supreme Jeymiyu called from the *forasa*.

Never let the woman lead them to the Supreme and twin Guides, neither of whom spoke. Could they speak? Either way, it seemed all was well, based on Jeymiyu's smile. Pleased. Pleased with himself.

"Once we arrive at the Eastern Palace, I would like to take a moment to show you one of the Living Wonders. We will then proceed to the Conclave, and thereafter, the Fountain."

Rikeva frowned. "A delay?"

"Yes. But once the Conclave's most pressing business is attended to, we will be summoned," Jeymiyu replied. "There is one further condition, actually."

"Being what, exactly?" she asked.

"As one of the Common People, you will need to bear a

mark while visiting any palace city."

"What mark?" She didn't seem as though she could be bothered challenging the man on 'Common People' and while it was not much better than 'lesser' or 'untamed', Never assumed that was the Amouni's attempt at being diplomatic.

Hubris, indeed.

Now, the young man seemed to hesitate. "A temporary branding that only appears while in a palace city."

"Find another way," Rikeva said.

"There is none," he replied. "I do apologise, but such laws are sacrosanct."

Never pointed at the Guardian. "You know we are only cooperating if Rikeva isn't harmed."

"She will be harmed *without* the mark, and none of us will be able to prevent it," Guardian Min replied. "I am meeting my obligations by urging you to allow this."

Never faced Rikeva. "Whatever you decide."

She smiled. "Thank you."

"If it allays your concerns," the Supreme said, "the mark is of light. Any Amouni can remove it once you leave the palace city – you will not experience discomfort."

"Describe this light," Rikeva said.

He spread his hands. "Merely a small bloom of red at your throat. Shaped as a joyous flower."

Never exchanged a glance with Rikeva and her expression matched his own – one of mild distaste, at best.

"I mean," Rikeva started with strained patience, "what does it mean for me to wear it?"

"You will be treated as Guest of a Subject."

"Suddenly, a little less poetic, aren't we?" Never said. And once more, he did not need a full answer from their escorts. Ecanseja's memories were enough. The city was rife with Subject-only places: taverns, smiths, healers, absolutely any and all aspects of commerce, and generally, day-to-day life.

Yet some Amouni would not even *speak* to those with the mark.

Other, worse hostilities existed; beatings and murders that were rarely investigated, let alone those responsible made to face justice.

"Her safety is assured with us. And of course, you yourself will be able to vouch for her should any challenge arise. Let us go to the *forasa*."

Now, Never frowned. "There is no rush, as you informed us. What challenges are you expecting?"

"None specific."

He sighed. "Supreme Jeymiyu –"

"Of course." The man ran a hand over his bald head. "I am not intending to hold things back but rather, I see no need to alarm you with the hypothetical."

"He is right, Never," the Guardian said. "Your true problems will only begin if the Conclave or the Fountain are unwilling to listen. You will be travelling with a Supreme and a Guardian. You yourself are Ascended. It is time to act on some faith."

"So be it," he replied after a moment. But he had one more question. "Are you permitted to join us, Guardian Min?"

"Of course."

"Are you not bound to your Temple?"

She regarded him with doubt and confusion once more, as though his question was quite odd. "It does not make sense that you would ask such a thing."

Never frowned. In Ecanseja's time, Temple Guardians *were* bound. Or, those at Temple Trivium were. Something was obviously going to change over the centuries. Or maybe some Guardians were bound and some were not... which meant there was every chance the man's memories might accidently steer him wrong at times.

"Wonderful. Please follow me," Supreme Jeymiyu said, taking Never's hesitation as acceptance, leading them toward the *forasa*.

Time to focus on escape.

Beside Never, Rikeva offered no objection as they walked – her faith in him more encouraging than Guardian Min's words. And maybe Rika was right to trust him, even in such an uncertain situation. The Amouni of the past were not aware of all that a mongrel could throw at them, if it came down to a fight.

Yet it seemed at least one more barrier would stand before them and progress toward returning home. An Amouni had landed before the *forasa* just as the Supreme set foot upon the symbol.

The newcomer was a well-built man in silver robes, his wings white and dusted in gold. A sneer upon his handsome face was the only response to Jeymiyu's polite request to use the symbol first. The newcomer wore a circlet and bracers with lattice-like patterns – obviously, someone high-ranking in a society already obsessed with status.

"I trust you'll understand," the Supreme said. "We have also arranged for limited permission for this travel, which will expire."

The man did not even take his gaze from the pair of Guides. "Guides, revoke permission. I will be travelling first."

The Guides did not respond with words, but the *forasa* brightened.

Guardian Min interrupted the Supreme's response. "Forgive us, Rahnzir. This is a matter of urgency."

Again, he did not bother to turn. "A pity, Guardian."

Never shoved the man aside. "Did no-one teach you manners?"

The Amouni stumbled, eyes bulging with outrage. Guardian Min and Supreme Jeymiyu both gasped, and despite the foolishness of it all, Never couldn't help but grin.

Rahnzir – or The Rahnzir, since it may have been a title – raised a burning hand to point. It was not of crimson-fire. Searing blue flame curled around his fingers as he clenched his fist. "Kneel for just punishment."

Never called his crimson-fire with a frown. "Do people here actually do that?"

"The intelligent ones."

The Amouni leapt forth, wings gleaming.

# Chapter 5.

Never caught the man's fist. Purple flames splashed without pain, as though both fires cancelled one another. For just a moment, the confrontation with Snow burned in his memory but in contrast, the snarling face before him now contained far more outrage than shock. As though not a single person had ever challenged this self-important fool. Not once, not in his entire life. A pathetic way to live, if true.

Never met the fellow's gaze. "Have you changed your mind?"

"What?" The Amouni spoke through clenched teeth.

"We're using the *forasa* now. Last chance to agree."

A blade appeared in the man's free grip; Never twisted his birch hand. Bone shattered. The crack echoed across the rooftop and the man collapsed to his knees. Blue flame vanished.

Never nudged the Amouni to one side before nodding to the others. "On to the Eastern Palace, then."

Or, Kiymako.

But when a speechless Supreme ushered him and Rikeva to the *forasa*, various apologies made by Guardian Min following, the silvery map Never had expected to appear within his mind was absent.

Instead, only a single bud – a pristine city seated upon golden plains. No walls to protect it. Instead, small towers had been placed at eight points of equal distance around the city's edge, these just as pale as the stone within.

Did the Amouni Eastern Palace rest somewhere in Marlosi's north?

He'd find out soon enough.

Light burned silver and gold, their destination appearing once the *forasa's* power faded.

Based on the smooth, pale walls and blue veins, it was yet another Temple interior. Although here, there was no additional light source, which gave the faces of his escorts a somewhat unpleasant pallor.

Or maybe that was just their expressions. Barely contained horror, for the most part. And maybe doubt, as once again it became clear the Amouni did not know all of which he was capable.

"Do you know who that was?" the Supreme asked, his voice risen in pitch.

"Rahnzir."

Guardian Min had folded her arms again. "You don't even know what that means, do you?"

"Not at all." Ecanseja's memories were of no help. "A prince or general? High Priest? Obviously, some manner of swine, based on his behaviour."

"No more insults," the Guardian said with an exasperated sigh. "And if you mean prince such as the Thanickanon have, then not precisely. A combination of prince and general, yes. But more importantly, each Rahnzir counts among the Conclave's most trusted envoys."

"I see." That could prove troublesome. "I hope he's a fast healer, like me."

Guardian Min turned away as if in further exasperation but had he caught just a hint of a smile as she moved?

The Supreme had raised an eyebrow. "He will recover, as I'm sure you know. How exactly did you do that?"

Never raised his birch hand, the bark-pattern dark in the poor light. "This one's stronger than it looks."

"Fascinating."

"Supreme, we must converse in private." Guardian Min was now frowning at them both.

"Certainly."

"Stay within," she told Never and Rikeva as the Amouni moved to step outside – the door having slid open quietly, and this time, a delicate handle was visible.

Once they were gone, Rikeva took his arm. "Never, you need to control your anger."

"Do I seem that angry?"

"No. But I know you are. And I know it's on my behalf, too."

"Not only – but of course, yes. These monsters need to treat you far better than this."

"You know I agree, but we still have to play by their rules until we know how to break them." She snickered then. "Even if it was worth seeing his face when you shoved him."

He chuckled. "You're right, I'm sorry. We don't know the rules here. I'll admit that… general or Rahnzir got under my skin, but the Conclave will be tempted by my blood, so I'm not worried about him interfering. I *am* irritated that the *forasa* was closed off. There was only one location, something I suspect our escorts arranged. Or it could be a customary thing, I've no idea."

"I don't think we can count the Rahnzir out just yet. You did break his hand."

Never chuckled. "He's probably more upset about his pride."

Rikeva punched his arm, and it seemed her patience was actually close to running out. "Stop it, fool."

"Very well."

"We need a new plan but it's near-impossible without knowing who controls what in this place. We need your hidden memories, Never."

"Sometimes general information simply isn't present. I assume because it's not important enough to form a lingering memory? Sometimes, it's not quite accurate, as I'm discovering. And I don't know when I'll 'remember' something either. At times, I just suddenly have some knowledge I didn't know I'd need."

"Anything at all now?"

He exhaled, beginning to pace. "Little of use. I mean, we know the Amouni are obsessed with hierarchy. We know they are deeply deluded or at best, preoccupied with 'purity'. We can assume that any magic or ability I have, they also possess, and likely more."

"To some extent, that seems true. But I think it's clear you would be able to surprise them."

"I'm betting on that."

"What about other lands? With the Amouni ruling everywhere, I assume, what does that mean for us if we reach Kiymako?"

He stopped to lean against the wall and nearly pushed himself back up again at a murmuring pulse within the blue beneath his back. Yet it caused no pain, seemed to offer no harm. "That, I think I can answer. Kiymako is a little more independent than other nations. Like the islands, actually."

Rikeva joined him and it seemed the blue veins had a similar, perhaps lesser effect on her. "That suits us."

"Thankfully. But the Amouni are still present there. It's just that I think more to trade and… travel for leisure, probably. Unlike in Hanik or Marlosi. The Amouni rule openly in most other places, or from the shadows via 'advisors'. Even the tribes bear some interference," he said.

Now, she frowned. "That's disappointing, even if I was expecting it. What else? What if we need to travel back to Vadiya?"

"In case the slaves of Arkenon hold some answers?"

"We shouldn't rule anything out."

"No, we shouldn't."

"I assume that's where the Amouni fight most of their battles? The Malecaphera."

"The Malecaphera. From what I can piece together, Vadiya's ancestors do still cause the Amouni trouble. Along with the Leschnilef. But I don't think we'll encounter those things. Mostly, it seems to be endless border skirmishes in Hanik, according to Ecanseja's memories. That, and occasional assassination attempts."

"Then if we are forced to escape on foot, who can we rely on?"

He shrugged. "Perhaps no-one. I'd rule out the Hanik,

since they are probably dutiful servants of the Amouni in this time."

"We're in Marlosi, at least." Then she shrugged. "For now."

"If we can communicate with the people outside the city, then we might be better accepted out there."

"This palace-city will be a big enough problem, I suppose." She sighed. "Which reminds me of something you said before, Never. You're confident this Conclave and the Fountain will want to use your blood. What if that isn't true? Or what if they simply decide they want to take it all, and then execute the both of us?"

"I know. I'm relying heavily on their wariness of me. And the Guardian's Oath."

"And?"

He laughed. "And… if it looks like I've got us in over our heads, then stand close by and I will burn our way free. I'm not totally certain, but I don't think the city is built to withstand the Phoenix's fire."

"In over our heads, yes." She placed one hand upon his cheek. "But it's not your fault that we're here, you know."

"Maybe."

"I'm serious. But I do have another question. What about *after* you burn a hole in every wall? What then?"

"I'll probably need you to carry me across the plain."

# Chapter 6.

When Supreme Jeymiyu and Guardian Min eventually re-entered the room, they were not alone.

A third, taller figure stood between them. Significantly taller, since their head nearly brushed the roof. But more striking was the fact that the newcomer had been draped from head to toe in white with an overlay of gold lace. There was no sense of how they might see or move without mishaps, but the head still turned to regard Never.

He could feel its eyes upon him – or its thoughts – seeking, trying to worm its way into his mind.

Never rebuffed it without knowing exactly how.

The figure did not react.

Guardian Min brought more light into the room via a pale flame she passed from hand-to-wall in order to brighten the white, allowing more detail upon the stranger to be revealed.

Faint runes were painted across the mouth.

Not impossible to read either, but their exact meaning was unclear. As best he could tell, the runes made a promise that all would be sheltered…

"Never. Rikeva," the Supreme said. "You are in the presence of Conclave Esuta, who was gracious enough to meet you directly, in a significant circumvention of convention."

"Is there an appropriate manner of address for us to use?" Never asked.

"Usually," Jeymiyu replied. "But her time is short. She will speak now. Merely stand as she reaches out – there is no danger."

Conclave Esuta glided near. The drapery trailed and as she stopped before them, she raised both hands, neither of which came free of the robes. The hand that landed on Never's shoulder seemed to carry more than the cloth's weight, fingers long and oddly warm.

*You have been permitted to carry out a task of great import. You must not fail.*

"Permitted, Conclave Esuta?" he asked, keeping his voice respectful. Rikeva was right. Best to play nice, especially with something he did not yet understand. Who knew what the strange woman before him was capable of?

*Along with your Untamed companion. Upon your successful return, you will be treated as Subjects, in spite of the questions surrounding your lineage.*

"Thank you." He ignored the fact that her answer had not been totally satisfactory. "What task are we to perform?"

*I leave the rest to the Supreme and Guardian.* She lifted her hand and with it, her voice was gone. Then, the robed figure glided toward the door, which opened before her touch.

Both Supreme Jeymiyu and Guardian Min bowed their heads, hands behind their backs as the Conclave member left.

"An explanation would be welcome," Never told them.

"It is simple enough," the Supreme replied. "We decided that, considering your blood, your story and your... irrepressible nature, that it would actually be best to approach the entire Conclave with an ally, along with a victory to share. Conclave Esuta is most amiable to this arrangement."

"So, she will speak on our behalf?" Rikeva asked.

"Once you return victorious."

"I have two concerns, as you might imagine," Never said. "What is she receiving from this arrangement? Not to mention each of you. And secondly, this task. Are we travelling into Vadiya? Is it the Malecaphera?"

The Supreme appeared to experience just a moment of confusion at the word 'Vadiya' but the use of 'Malecaphera' on its heels seemed to clear things up. "You will not be sent west, no."

Guardian Min continued. "There is an uprising underway in the far east. Beyond the Sol Seas, on the Spring Colony. That is where we will be travelling."

Now he had yet more questions. One being about the supposed lands beyond the Sol Seas, lands that did not exist in his time, but it would have to wait.

By Rikeva's expression, she had questions too. "You're joining us?"

"Only I," the Guardian replied. "Supreme Jeymiyu must attend to other matters."

"That leads me back to my previous question," Never said. "What do you all hope to gain from this?"

"I have an Oath to uphold," Guardian Min replied. "In addition, my standing in society will be raised considerably once we succeed."

"As will mine," Supreme Jeymiyu added. Once again, his somewhat treacle-laden smile returned. "Those with the Conclave's favour experience privilege, luxury and comfort that few even glimpse."

Never exchanged a glance with Rikeva. If nothing else, the Amouni were certainly up front about their opportunistic reasons. Almost matter-of-fact. Yet more proof they were not only untrustworthy but perhaps deserving of their eventual fates.

"Why don't we continue this discussion over a meal?" the Supreme suggested. "Even a Temple offers exquisite fare."

Never gestured for the man to lead the way.

The corridor beyond was similar, save for another pair of mute Guides flanking the door, and stretched toward a distant, quite conventional-seeming lamp. They passed several stairways, each well-lit, this time via filtered light from quartz. Most veins were a pale blue, but here they stood closer to columns within the walls rather than the thinner veins that had appeared earlier.

When his escorts opened a door beside the lamp, it was to reveal yet another plain room. This time, however, six chairs of snowy white were arranged at a long table. Its steel surface gleamed with cleanliness, like everything else so far.

Just one painting and a square of quartz, facing one another from opposite walls. The painting was of yet another race, only this time with wings through the sky. Not a single plant or scrap of coloured fabric… and something about the sameness to it all began to grate upon Never. Even the buried city beneath the Folhan Ranges had offered more variety.

Still, it was just two Temple interiors he'd seen. Perhaps the Amouni did have some imagination when it came to architecture and decoration, and it would be revealed elsewhere.

Once seated, the Supreme called for a Guide – this one bearing the head of a cat – and requested food and drink. "It will arrive shortly," he replied.

"What of Conclave Esuta, then?" Never asked. "To what other heights can she climb?"

"Only one," Guardian Min replied. "The Fountain."

"To usurp?"

"No. That is not the way it works," Guardian Min replied, and now *she* exchanged a glance with her companion. "Again, I am impressed by your dedication to your story – or concerned that it is true."

"I am curious. For what purpose do you imagine I would need to lie?"

"To explain away the fil… the impurities in your blood. Deceiving everyone might permit you full participation in society, something I assume you have not enjoyed. Your Blood speaks of years denied the shelter offered by your people. Supreme?"

The young man nodded. "That is my assessment also. With such a wide range of contaminants, he is either a masterful criminal the likes of which has not been seen in all our lives, or he is telling the truth."

Never raked his gaze from one to the other. "Would you like to find some strangers from the Temple to insult me, too? Any friends or family near a *forasa* that you could call upon?"

"You cannot deny that –"

Never raised a hand, aware of Rikeva's frown. "Very well. Let me ask you one final question about my blood, instead. Do you truly believe the Great Phoenix would have blessed me, if I were not honest?"

Silence met his words.

Rikeva leant across the table. "Even if you don't yet believe us, we are *not* from this age. And we mean to return home as soon as possible but that doesn't mean we cannot help each other first."

"Ah, well said, Rikeva of Marlosi," the Supreme replied. "To that end, why don't I explain a little more about your task?"

"An uprising in your Spring Colony?" Never asked.

"It is often the way with the Common Peoples," he replied with a rather paternal sigh, a sound somehow all the more unpleasant by his relative youth. "We have shown them a virtuous path yet still they choose violence at every opportunity."

"Their grievance?"

"A misguided desire for self-governance, among other things. Trifling quibbles over taxation."

"How rude of them."

"Understand, we have improved their lives in every conceivable way. You will see for yourself when you arrive. Min?"

"He is right," she added. "I have visited the colony several times."

A veritable expert, then. "Tell us more about the people there."

"Common, of course," Guardian Min said. "They have long-resisted our bounty in full. The Conclave once believed the influence of the Malecaphera but that has recently come into doubt. Their resistance to Amouni gifts is more likely innate, in part due to their diet, which changed after a great tragedy."

"What tragedy?"

"Something colossal fell from the sky. It struck the colony with such force that half an entire forest was flattened, along with a few villages. The true tragedy was a research group working to gather plant-life for medicinal purposes. They, too, were lost. This was five decades past, now."

Their conversation was interrupted by the arrival of food, which included pale yellow roots partially covered in a tomato-seeming sauce. It was delicious, as were the varied meat and vegetables, boasting immaculate seasoning.

Yet Never noted that after they had finished a subtle dessert, Rikeva reached for her stomach a moment. While the Amouni spoke to the Hanik servants who had come to take away the plates, he checked on her, but she only smiled. "I'm fine."

Her expression suggested a little too much doubt.

But with the return of their escorts, there was no time to ask more questions.

# Chapter 7.

Once the plates and cutlery had been cleared away, Rikeva addressed the Guardian and Supreme. "What else can you tell us? So far, we don't even know the colony's name."

"But you do – it is the Spring Colony," Supreme Jeymiyu replied.

"No, I mean its real name," she said. "How do the locals refer to their land? And themselves, for that matter."

He looked to the Guardian. "I am afraid I do not recall."

"A moment." She closed her eyes. "Ah. It was Aratho; I believe the people there use a variant on that word to describe themselves... Arathona. No doubt the rebels will use something of the like, too."

It seemed Rikeva wanted to share her thoughts on such a revelation but she was better at controlling her tongue than Never. Still, he managed to ask a useful question, instead of saying something sarcastic as he'd wanted. "I assume you know from where the rebels operate?"

"Largely. Our scouts found evidence within the wilds."

"And they outnumber you?"

"Likely, yes. Not always a problem, and we do have a garrison stationed at the capital, along with the typical web of *forasa* and Guides, but the Spring Colony has a dampening effect on our birthright. I mentioned their resistance to our gifts."

"Not rendering them useless, of course," the Supreme added. "But enough that the Rahnzir has requested more assistance."

"Which is where we become useful."

"Perhaps instrumental," the Guardian replied. "Based on what I have already learnt from your blood, I am not expecting you to experience the same difficulties there."

The door slid open to reveal a barefoot Amouni. The man was dressed in nothing but white pants. His muscled chest bore the tattoo of a stretching figure, and he inclined his head to the other Amouni before addressing them. "Forgive my interruption. Conclave Esuta has assigned me to provide your guests with an escort to the Grand Bazaar. She suggests you all take this time to prepare for your respective duties until the morrow."

"Tomorrow, when we are due to depart?" the Guardian asked.

"Yes."

"Wonderful." She stood. "We can finish sharing what we know in the carriage. Never, Rikeva, please follow this guard and purchase whatever you may need. You may return to the Temple or take accommodation at any of the inns. Be warned, not all will accept Rikeva."

"I see." Never hesitated. "And that is all? You don't wish to accompany us?"

Supreme Jeymiyu himself appeared somewhat concerned, since his smile had faded and the man was poised to speak.

But the Guardian answered first. "You may consider this a sign of my commitment to developing the trust needed for us to work together on a dangerous journey."

"And if I want to consider it a test?"

"You may do so."

Fleeing was not necessarily off the table, but there was an increasing likelihood that cooperating at least a little longer would end up being worthwhile. Without fully trusting them, of course. "I appreciate that. If we choose to stay in the city, I assume we meet here to travel to Atharo?"

"This or another *forasa*. But unless anything changes, start here after dawn."

Before they left, the Supreme affixed the mark of light to Rikeva, and as promised, it was a fairly elegant, rose-like glow. Clearly visible to any that sought it, but not in danger of becoming a light source in and of itself.

Even so, Rikeva frowned as the guard led them from the room, down the corridors and from the temple via a minor exit, moving with efficient swiftness.

Outside, the surrounding streets were uncluttered – in every sense of the word. The occasional stone bench, a few lone trees whose shade spread far and wide, but equally, trees that could have been illusory, since he could not see a single stray leaf upon the ground. More, only one person approached the Temple entrance, with what seemed to be a broken wing, based on the bandages.

Why were they healing so slowly?

Or maybe it wasn't broken at all. A disease? Once again, Ecanseja's memories stepped in to provide answers; the bandaged wing was to be groomed within the Temple. A sign of vanity, then.

"Never of the Ascended, and companion," the new guard said. "Conclave Esuta has arranged for your purchases. Please continue to follow me."

Never nodded – he must have stopped walking.

In the light of day, it was easier to see that the servant carried a long dagger of blue – and by the way the weapon called, it was clearly just as dangerous as the ones that took Mondesa and Sirgeto during the invasion.

Not that the weapon seemed necessary. The palace-city really was quiet. Few servants or Amouni moved about as they walked, passing the smooth, pale stone or steel of the buildings, and occasional fountains or little gardens. The lawns inside appeared to have been built large enough for four or five people to enjoy at the most.

Once, they walked beneath a bridge that spanned the buildings, its supports casting long shadows, and their guard stopped.

Before Never could ask what was amiss, he saw it himself.

A shadow that leapt between shadows.

Just like Ivadr – Malecaphera!

Never called his crimson-fire and shot forward, hands ablaze, but the shadow had already flitted up toward the underside of the bridge to vanish within. He glanced back to their guard. "Do we give chase?"

"No. I will inform the nearest Guardian. As a guest of the Eastern Palace, you are not expected to labour so."

And so they continued on, soon finding the Grand Bazaar.

It was grand in scale, though like the rest of the place, seemed far too quiet. For a market that spanned most of a city square, it featured but two dozen stalls, and only four people were out shopping. Three were Amouni – a woman and her two children – and the other appeared to be a Marlosi servant or visitor, dressed in far more colourful garb.

While stalls sold a range of food, clothing, weapons and other items that ought to have been of interest to the citizens, there was simply no bustle; no voices haggling, just soft words exchanged in the calm.

"I have other matters to attend to," their escort said before turning to leave. "Please take all the time you may need here."

Once the man was gone, Never glanced around. "What do we need?"

Rikeva folded her arms. "Packs and flasks. Blankets. Some travel rations, I suppose."

"You don't seem impressed."

"Are you?"

"Actually, in a way – I wasn't certain I could be surprised again, but it's almost as if the Amouni are simply very, very private, or that their numbers are few. Far fewer than I imagined possible. This is supposed to be a city."

"We can use that to our advantage," she said. "Let's go."

They found what they needed quickly, the stallholders supplying everything at the mention of Conclave Esuta. He'd spent only a little extra time with a woman who was selling weapons.

There, while he replenished his supply of daggers, the children approached. They held a dark puppy, smiling and laughing together. And while neither had much to say, even when he knelt to return their greeting, they seemed pleased enough to have seen him up close, even squealing as they returned to their mother's robes. Never smiled at the woman too… only for it to fade.

The Amouni wore an expression of distaste as she regarded Rikeva.

Rikeva merely grinned back, as if daring the Amouni to speak. Which, of course, she did not, ushering her children away. Never watched them leave, struck by the unpleasant knowledge that the children would grow up to be like their mother, taught to believe other people were beneath them.

Never and Rika left the Bazaar and found seats in the nearest garden. Its scattered vegetation provided just enough shade, yet even here there was little colour; the bark was grey on the saplings and the modest flowerbed bore only blue and white blossoms. When Never leant forward to check their scent, it seemed the flowers shrank away… because he was blocking the setting sun?

A bird lurked somewhere in the leaves above – a faint flutter of wings, but it did not sing.

"Did you notice how quiet the city is?" Rikeva asked. "Everywhere we went, just a hush."

Nearby, two robed figures strode together, speaking softly. Despite the proximity to such a central part of the city, no-one else was out and about. "I did. Those children laughing was the loudest thing."

"It's unnaturally clean, too," she added.

"I don't mind that aspect, myself."

Rika nudged him in the rib. "Neither do I, under normal circumstances." She leant both elbows upon her knees, closing her eyes. "But even with the Guides, most of the work is done by unhappy 'Common People', I suspect."

"Likely, yes."

Rikeva sighed. "And us? I know we can't trust the Amouni, but will we be safe in one of their inns? Rooms in the Temple will have too many spies."

"Truly. But I do think we will be safe. After all, we're too important now."

"*You* are, Never."

He nodded. "Sorry, you're right. We'll sleep in shifts, and I'll set a ward."

"Is that possible?"

"Thanks to Ecanseja," he said with a nod. "He has something worth trying. I can't be certain, but I now think I have a better idea of where some of the pieces are fitting. Time-wise."

"Do you mean that he was nearer to our day?"

"Yes, which makes some of his tricks unknown *here*."

"That's good enough for me," Rikeva said as she stood and stretched. "Ready?"

Never joined her, and together they walked the empty streets. The homes they passed bore windows empty of curtains, but windows that were still difficult to see beyond. A strong need for privacy?

They soon came to an inn – recognisable only by its name and by the large windows on the third and fourth storey. "Let's try this one," Never said as they entered.

Inside, a sparrow-head Guide greeted them. It stood in a white room with a large, closed door at its back. *Master. Do you wish for a meal or a room?*

"Both." Never reached for his purse… would they take unfamiliar currency? Had the Conclave arranged for their room, also?

*We can offer both. However, your guest must eat alone.*

"We will find another inn."

Rikeva rested a hand on his arm. "Never, I'd prefer we eat in our room, actually."

Perhaps that would be better; he should have realised. "Where is the owner?" he asked the Guide.

*Beyond. Please enter.*

The door slid open, revealing the first use of colour upon any walls that seemed purposeful decoration. Someone had painted pink and grey patterns, as if to adorn the place with grey branches and pink blossoms.

Quite a pleasant reception. Two archways led to a quiet dining area with tables and chairs, and to something of a lounge, featuring only divans and armchairs. And here, too, the coloured upholstery caught his eye more than the Amouni in their robes.

They sipped at thick liquors of gold and pink, and those that bothered to look over their drinks, did so with some distaste.

"Good evening," said an Amouni woman as she approached. "Can I provide a discreet room?"

Unlike the others, her robe was short enough to reveal her knees, along with calf-high boots of a swirling design – one that was matched upon her long gloves. Her smile was welcoming, but it did not reach her eyes. A rather common occurrence amongst the Amouni.

"You assume that, why?"

The woman glanced to Rikeva. "Your Untamed Mistress, of course."

Rikeva folded her arms, and Never turned to face her – speaking in Marlosi, now. "We really can seek another inn."

"They will all be the same. At least this one claims to offer something discreet."

He nodded. Never switched back to Amouni, addressing the owner once more. "Discreet is fine."

She frowned, and it seemed she wanted to ask about the Marlosi words, obviously being unable to understand. Which was interesting. And useful. But in the end, the innkeeper only gestured to a large staircase already being revealed behind her, as another wall slid open. There, a desk also waited. "Conclave Esuta has informed the Guides that your stay is without cost and that you are to be treated as honoured guests. She will also send someone in the morning."

"We are in her debt," he said.

Upstairs, they walked a spacious corridor lit by generous windows and the setting sun, whose soft orange rays slipped between buildings. At the third door, their host pressed a panel. It slid open without blood, and she gestured inside. "I will send for a meal. The kitchen boasts Chef Otajou, you will be pleased to know."

Never kept a sarcastic comment to himself. "Will we have time to bathe first?"

"In the third chamber," she said, starting back toward the stair. "Make sure you set the door."

While Rikeva slumped into the nearest armchair, Never pressed his finger against the panel. The door slid closed. Did it need blood? Or was he now the only one able to use it? Assuming that was what the owner meant when she told him to 'set' the door. "Remind me to have you test this later," he said to Rikeva.

She nodded, slinging one leg across the armrest, her eyes closed.

"Tired?"

"It's exhausting."

"Being treated like –"

"– Like I am inferior," she said, finishing his sentence.

"I can set the ward now and we can skip the meal, if you like?"

"Tempting." She smiled as she sat up, then rose to head for the next room. "But let's take everything they offer and more – starting with a bath."

"Need me to join you?" he asked with a grin.

"It's too small," she called back, the click of a door sliding shut following.

## Chapter 8.

While Rikeva bathed, Never attempted to unearth more of Ecanseja's memories.

Ultimately, they remained unpredictable. Both in terms of when *and* whether they would appear. And when he did come across something relevant, it wasn't always revealed in detail. Some things didn't match exactly what Never saw or encountered, and no-one could ask a memory for clarity.

Worse, he was increasingly discovering that the Guardian's memories were sometimes incomplete or even contradictory.

He *did* discover a few useful things from where he lay across a divan, but spent an equal amount of time going over the Blood Ward, a seal he would enact later, which was a simple enough process.

Or so it seemed, without having actually attempted one.

When Rikeva rejoined him, she appeared much refreshed; her golden curls vibrant and her eyes almost sparkling. "Your turn – and I won't spoil the surprise, but it's quite impressive."

"Finally, something to look forward to in this place."

He stood, but a chiming of bells rang in the room.

Never crossed the carpet and pressed the panel to reveal a servant with a large tray of covered dishes. The young man wore a short robe the colour of fading grass, woollen in texture and in marked contrast to the more silken robes of the Amouni.

"Your meal is ready." The lad bore an accent – most likely Hanik. "There is also a note for you from Lady Linjamet." The servant gestured between dishes to a piece of folded parchment. "I can serve and take the tray as I leave, if you wish," he added.

Never lifted the note. "That would be welcome."

He read the message from Linjamet while the servant went to work in the dining room.

*If you wish to farm your Untamed One please contact me. This inn will expect a higher than average commission. However, you will always be able to charge more for Untamed.*

Never blinked, then read the note again. No mistake. His hand shook, but he managed not to crumple the message. Instead, he rummaged around within a nearby desk, finding a quill and ink to write his response.

I will tear the wings from your body if you mention 'farming' again. If you do not have wings, I will drown you in the nearest fountain.

"Never?" Rikeva called.

"On my way." He folded the paper and joined her and

the servant. The young man stood back from the table, tray in hand, waiting for the message. And it seemed that despite himself, the lad had been glancing often to the food, which was another lovely mix of meats, vegetables and more delicious, soft vegetable root. All of which had been lavishly sauced.

Never smiled at him. "Take whatever you wish."

"My Lord?"

Never sat beside Rikeva. "I am not trying to ensnare you, if that is your fear. Please eat. Something caught your eye, didn't it?"

"Well… the fire-dumplings. But only if you are certain?"

Rikeva lifted the plate with a smile.

The servant started to eat, cheeks soon bulging. "Thank you, both," he said when finished.

Never handed over the message. "Before you deliver this, I would like your opinion. If the owner reads this, will you face her ire simply for being the one to deliver it?"

The servant unfolded the parchment and read, eyes widening as a range of emotions ran across his face – concern, shock and then what could have been… joy? Or perhaps even gratitude?

"No. She is not so bad as others."

"Good. Please deliver her my response."

He nodded and strode from their chambers with a smile that he would hopefully be able to control by the time he found Linjamet.

Rikeva paused with a fork half-way to her mouth. "What was that about?"

"The innkeeper offered something and I refused."

"Exactly how impolite were you?"

"Downright threatening."

She set her fork down. "Never."

"We are Conclave Esuta's honoured guests, remember?" He crammed some of the chicken into his mouth. "Trust me. They wouldn't dare act against the hierarchy."

"Your ill-mannered assurances aside, I think you should tell me."

He swallowed the rest of his mouthful. "Apparently, Amouni inns double as brothels – or at least partners to them, since she asked if I wanted to sell you for the night. But don't worry, we could have charged a higher price because you are 'Untamed'. Charming, aren't they?"

She leant back in her chair, a dark expression on her face. "I see."

"Let's finish the meal and I'll seal us in for the night."

Rikeva nodded, then reached out to place her hand over his own. "I think my appetite is disappearing."

"Take the bed. I'll create the Blood Ward once I'm done here."

She went to the bedroom and Never finished the last of the meal, the vegetables a little less wonderful than expected. "Sorry, Chef Otajou." Not good enough to counter the bitter taste that lingered after the innkeeper's note.

Once he'd finished and tidied up as best he could, he tucked two spoons into a pocket and returned to the entryway. There, he drew his dagger and made twin incisions in his palms. Not needed in order to call crimson-fire, but sometimes the ritual seemed fitting.

The memory of Ecanseja guided him. He gripped both spoons and let them melt. The crimson globes of flame turned a dark silver, bloody embers flickering inside. Never sprayed a thin line around the doorway, hissing following his movements, and then strode across the room to repeat the process with each window.

Rikeva rose from the bed when he sealed the bedroom window. "Will you need to maintain it, somehow?"

"Not according to Ecanseja. I believe it's mostly the blood, with the steel being partially symbolic."

She lay back down, hands behind her head. "Either way, I suppose you're right about the Conclave. If they want to use us, there's no need for them to attack. Attackers would likely be another Malecaphera."

"Hopefully not. Do you need anything else?"

Rikeva laughed. "Stop fussing, Never. I'm just going to get some rest. I don't know if the food here agrees with me, to be honest. Otherwise, I'd ask you to join me."

He paused, a thrill charging through his body. "Oh?"

"Of course. But tonight, I'm afraid you'll have to make do with the floor. Or one of the divans."

"And now I have something to look forward to before heading home."

"So do I. Now get out and let me sleep."

He laughed as he closed the door.

## Chapter 9.

When Guardian Min met them in the reception area the next morning, after a thankfully uneventful night – though one filled with a certain longing – the innkeeper was no-where to be seen.

She'd obviously taken his message to heart. As well she ought.

Less pleasing was a somewhat pale tint to Rikeva's complexion, though she'd assured him she was well. It certainly didn't prevent her from carrying her staff or pack.

"Further provisions are due to arrive momentarily," the Guardian said as she led them out into the street. Once again, despite what ought to have been a busy morning typical of a city, there was just a hush. Occasional small groups of Amouni walked together. Servants moved a little quicker, but even they hardly filled the streets.

Nor did wagons or horses, nor any other beast of burden for that matter.

"Will your servants accompany us to Aratho?" Never asked.

"No. We three alone," she replied as a set of footsteps

neared – another muscled Guard arriving with two small purses and a pair of collars. He handed them over without a word then set off at a jog.

Guardian Min explained the contents. "A small amount of coin each, and a collar. I have also been permitted to imbue your weapons should you decide you need that."

Never glanced up from where he'd been examining the coins, of an even size but varying colours – greens, blues and yellows. "We will forgo that, I believe. Unless you think we'll encounter the Leschnilef somewhere in Aratho?"

"I do not expect to. They have not been encountered beyond the Arafolhanim Ranges in decades, and have been driven deep beneath the mountain now. Their numbers are quite close to extinction."

"Sadly, they will survive for a good many centuries to come."

She met his gaze. "You know that to be true?"

"Firsthand."

Rikeva lifted the collar, a brilliant blue lined in steel. "What is the purpose of this? Another tool to be used to mark me as inferior?"

"No." Guardian Min seemed to welcome the distraction from what Never had revealed. She gestured to her own collar. "Never and I will also wear one, though I do not believe he will require it. The collar will protect you from the aftermath of the tragedy."

"Exactly how does it work? We still don't know much about what happened."

"I will explain more when we enter the forests. For now, we must move swiftly if we don't wish to miss our scheduled use of the *forasa*."

Never sighed. "Using the *forasa* was much more fun when I could do it at will."

The woman slowed. "Are you claiming that you did not have to wait? That it wasn't necessary to submit a request in advance?"

"Of course not." He shrugged. "And who would I submit it to? There's no-one left."

Pain flashed across her face then. "Oh."

He couldn't stop a stab of guilt – and why not? Tormenting her wasn't needed, even if he hadn't intended to do so. "I know you're finding it hard to believe me. To believe the memories and history you witnessed in my blood, but our time is *very* different."

She waved a hand. "No. If I am to accept what seems to be true, I need to confront the possibilities, however dark."

He did not add that the things he shared were not *possibilities.*

"Where is our *forasa?*" Rikeva asked. "Back at the Temple?"

"There is one closer," Min said as she set off. "At the southern gate, a short walk."

Never followed, Rikeva at his side. And the Guardian was not wrong, since they reached the gate after crossing a few streets only.

Yet it was not a gate that controlled entry into the palace-city, but a towering arch of black stone wide enough for a pair of carts to pass through. A shining *forasa* spanned the arch, flanked by eight of the identical Guides.

A pair of Amouni stood waiting, their heads close together as they spoke softly.

They did not turn when Guardian Min arrived, but one

did unfold a set of dark wings as a Guide beckoned them closer. A short conversation followed, one that to Never sounded quite formal, then they stepped into the symbol and vanished.

Yet the Guides permitted access without hesitation when the Guardian approached.

This time when he stepped through the symbol and the light rose and faded, it was to find himself in an entirely different city.

A city full of sound, movement, and colour.

A city of life.

He had not been told the name of what was likely Aratho's capital, but it was clearly more than pale white walls and quartz. It was… almost like being home, in some ways.

Thanks to the voices.

Mostly those speaking an unfamiliar language, but the meanings were clear enough –frustration in an argument between two merchants over who would unload before a nearby warehouse first. Children laughing as they pestered one of the guards, clambering up to reach for the bright fruit. A young couple before a tavern, the woman staring at her shoes, a little unsteady where she endured being scolded by her husband.

Both wore dark clothing with coloured ribbons tied at the sleeves. The man also wore a scarf, in an echo of what was fashionable in the Hanik port of Lenan. Here, however, the scarf seemed to be built to cover the entire face like a mask, with eyeholes filled by resin, something Never noted when another local passed by, the scarf-mask covering his face.

"We helped create them to protect people during the storms," the Guardian said. "But still they are not satisfied with all that we do."

He glanced up at morning light where it fell across the surrounding buildings. Their tiled rooves were mostly black, shaped as sweeping triangles, walls of painted wood and stone, in marked contrast to Amouni construction. "Are we due to meet a commander here? Or the local puppet?"

She frowned. "Yes. Rahnzir Bixuhol. The 'puppet' as you claim, is Queen Ilekah. She has long been a valuable ally to the Amouni when it comes to preventing war. Especially within the Colony itself."

"Between whom?" Rikeva asked.

"The Aratho and mountain folk to the east."

"Are we on a path to become involved with any of those battles? I don't relish the idea of being caught between rebels and a second threat." Never tapped the collar at his throat. "Third, if you count whatever these collars protect against."

Guardian Min shook her head. "Our path lies to the north. We will take a carriage to the keep."

"Does that mean you've already arranged…" Never trailed off as the sound of hooves on cobblestones reached him. She obviously had.

Four horses drew a carriage constructed in a wave-like shape, though its wooden panels and wheels were painted black and grey. Even the horses' tack matched. The carriage stopped beside the tavern. Muttering followed the Guardian as she climbed in, and Never glanced at the angry faces lining the tavern's windows before joining her.

"Popular, aren't we?"

"Nothing will come of it," she replied.

A whip cracked and the carriage lurched into motion, wheels rattling over stone. Never stared out the window as the buildings began to change – fewer inns, and more merchants with colourful signs appearing as they neared the keep.

"I don't see a lot of weapons here. What do the Aratho favour?" he asked after a time.

"It varies across the regions and cities. Bows. Darts and blow guns. Swords too, sometimes."

"I see. And do you carry any weapons beyond our gifts and that knife?"

"Just the dagger, though less than you."

"But I won't be tipping the balance with steel."

"No," she replied, then pointed through the window. "There's the keep."

Stretching above the high walls, which also bore dark tiles and openings for archers, was the keep. Almost a peak in and of itself. The lower storeys covered several blocks in dark stone, with the upper being similar if smaller, all fortified by small catapults.

Yet by the top of the keep, the final graceful peak was no more than a single room – no doubt also containing a look-out.

"Impressive."

"Another example of Amouni working with the Common Peoples," the Guardian said with a pleased nod.

"Something that can no longer be done?" Rikeva asked.

"Are you asking about the rebellion?"

"Yes."

"They have spurned many offers of peace. I do not believe

they will negotiate in good faith." She paused. "Queen Ilekah and Rahnzir Bixuhol will be expecting us to break the rebellion by force – were you not aware of that?"

"And if we want to try negotiation first?"

Their escort spread her hands. "I cannot speak for the Queen, nor the Rahnzir. But I will follow their orders, and if you wish to have the full cooperation of the Conclave, you must do the same."

# Chapter 10.

Queen Ilekah sat in a bright hall, curtains tied open by golden rope that let morning light stream within. It spilled across the marble floor leading to her throne… which was unusually soft – being as it was an armchair. Even more unusual, the chair had been tilted slightly forward, with the back legs resting upon a slab of marble.

Or perhaps it was not unusual, for Queen Ilekah appeared quite old. Her face was wrinkled, white hair in disarray and her gaze drifting. An ornate cane lay across her lap, half-concealed by the folds of a pink shawl.

A stout man wearing a dark, oversized coat with large, painted buttons stood beside the armchair-throne, and it was he who responded to Guardian Min's formal introductions. "Welcome, all. Queen Ilekah is most pleased that you are able to assist." His accent was light, a subtle elongation of the Amouni words.

The Queen offered a benevolent smile only.

Guardian Min inclined her head before turning back to the advisor. "Is the Rahnzir joining us?"

"Alas, his replacement is being arranged as we speak."

Now she frowned. "Replacement? Gillori, what has happened?"

"Ah, yes." Gillori's expression became troubled. "It appears that only last night, one of the Shades metamorphosed with a cloud of Seeds. Most regrettably, Rahnzir Bixuhol was among those lost. The Conclave is sending another –"

"I'm responsible for the new dam in the hills, you know." Queen Ilekah's voice cut through the man's explanation, bright and cheery. "It saved a lot of my people."

Gillori leant down. "You did, Your Majesty. It was a fine day." His tone was patient without being patronising. "Would you lend us your insights today, also?"

She blinked. "Oh, I'm not sure I'd be of much use."

"It is most pressing, My Queen."

"If you say so," she said, and settled back within the chair, closing her eyes. She tapped gnarled fingers upon her cane. "Did you arrange for little Syvame to get her dress adjusted?"

"Of course."

"Good, good," the Queen said, and the tapping of her fingers slowed as she appeared to slip into a peaceful doze.

"Advisor Gillori." Guardian Min's frown had only deepened. "When were you planning to reveal the extent of Her Majesty's decline?"

He spread both hands. "I assumed that the Rahnzir had been providing such reports. It is a natural progression of a long process, after all."

"From where I stand, it appears to be a rapid decline."

"Her Majesty is far more lucid after meals."

"In the meantime, I will require more information about recent events. Is there somewhere we could wait for the Rahnzir's replacement?"

"Certainly." He gestured to a doorway leading to shadowy halls. "The first room within will be sufficient. I must arrange for Her Majesty's care now, but I imagine that the new Rahnzir will have arrived before I rejoin you."

"Very well." She gestured for Never and Rikeva to follow.

Her footfalls were sharp as she led them across the marble and into the hallway.

Never glanced back, and both advisor and queen were now speaking softly; her movements decisive and a cunning glint in her gaze. Never couldn't help a smile; it seemed Queen Ilekah was not in such a state of decline after all.

Nor, perhaps, the staunch ally the Amouni had long-counted on.

The room Advisor Gillori had suggested was lit only by a single lamp, but it also featured a generous skylight, offering plenty of illumination. Here, no more marble. Instead, polished floorboards and a circle of cushioned chairs.

And that was the last of the furniture.

"No table?" Never asked as he took a chair, Rikeva settling in beside him.

The Guardian sat opposite. "It is a custom in the Spring Colony for meetings to be short and focused. No distractions from food or drink that may be set upon a table."

"Interesting."

She nodded shortly, as though she had not truly heard his response. Her gaze seemed to have been drawn to the door. And when she stood, she revealed the reason. "The new Rahnzir will join us in a moment. I ask that you control your baser instincts, Never."

"I'm not going to proposition whoever it is, if that's what you're suggesting."

"I am not talking about your libido."

The door opened to reveal a familiar, sneering face – the Rahnzir whose hand Never had broken at the Temple. He still wore silver robes and circlet, his arms, which he folded, remained adorned in lattice-work bracers.

"Oh. You meant my temper."

"She did," the Rahnzir replied. "Allow me to make that easier for you, should you be able. I am Rahnzir Sarion and I am most keen to cooperate on this vital task."

"That is heartening, Rahnzir," Never replied, instead of a comment about the man's manners being much improved. Not enough that the fellow appeared likely to give an apology for his past behaviour, but it was better than nothing. "Know that Rikeva and I will do what we can to assist you and the Conclave."

"Wonderful." He sat beside Min, adjusting the chair a little with his hands – both of which appeared perfectly fine. "First, a question regarding social order, along with command, must be satisfied."

"Your seniority is clear, Rahnzir," Guardian Min said.

"However, not for Never. I have taken time to review your initial report on his blood and am not satisfied that he is only Ascended."

"Of course," the Guardian replied. "It is difficult to say, and a matter I hoped the Conclave would choose to solve."

"As I am sure they will, in time. For the purposes of this undertaking, I wish to come closer to a resolution."

Never glanced between them. "To what end?"

Rahnzir Sarion's frown revealed his confusion. "All of life is about understanding one's place."

A likely answer from an Amouni. "Even if you can conclusively prove to the Conclave where I may or may not fit in the social hierarchy in this age, how will it help quell this rebellion?"

"It allows me to understand who you might be able to command, should another tragedy befall us in the coming days. And afterward, if needed."

Rikeva gave the man a look. "You cannot be suggesting that the other Amouni will fall under Never's authority."

"That is exactly what I am suggesting," he replied with a short nod. "Lives are saved when there are no doubts over chain of command."

"Possibly," Never replied. "But you know that my cooperation is conditional. If I believe the Conclave is no longer intending to help me, then I feel no obligation."

"Then let us settle your standing, so that you might be guaranteed that assistance."

# Chapter 11.

Never regarded the man with a new doubt. What exactly did the Amouni want, and how did it differ from what everyone else sought? "Forgive me, but that sounds like the words of a long-time ally, and we have only met twice. Further, that first meeting gave me cause to doubt your character."

"Understandable," the man replied, and it seemed he was fighting to control his own temper – at the slight? "But my motives are not so hard to understand. Simply put, I do not want you here."

Never raised an eyebrow. "A clear motive, indeed."

"You represent a troubling contradiction."

"Do I?"

He leant back. "Yes. On the one hand, you are a colossal threat to the natural order of not only Amouni society, but all lands. To the very fabric of our lives. Your arrival may well herald the end of everything we fought to create, meaning that you must be returned immediately."

"And the other hand?"

"A singular chance for a very different tomorrow."

"Flattering. But you've admitted that you believe the former."

"Without question." He shrugged. "Yet, what if I am wrong? If that is the case, I would give you every chance to make those changes. First here in the Colony, should I also fall in battle, and secondly, if needed, beyond this conflict."

"A significant responsibility."

"However, unless I am convinced of that unlikely outcome, I mean to use your abilities here and now with the rebellion only. Afterwards, I will send you home, however that may be possible."

"That would be wonderful," Never replied. Yet, surely there was something more afoot? The Amouni had other, deeper motives, and the very open discussion of obvious ones was no guarantee of them being the *only* factors at play.

The problem was discovering what was hidden.

It always was.

Guardian Min did not seem pleased with the general's speech. "Rahnzir, while I find it useful to learn that you have come to a conclusion about his blood, there is no guarantee that anything we uncover about Never while on this task will be accepted by all."

"Not by all, but Conclave Esuta is not alone in her interest in this man."

"Conclave Yigiwa?"

"Yes. Among others, as I understand it. They are awaiting the outcome of our actions here in the Colony."

More wonderful news. "Thrilling to know that I now have such unwavering support."

"I see." Guardian Min rubbed at her temples a moment, before asking another question of the Rahnzir. "In what scenario do you envision Never commanding our party?"

Never raised a hand. "Before you answer, you might as well give us an overview. I'll need to know who I outrank, if you are serious about all this."

"I assume that even in your time, it begins as follows," Rahnzir Sarion replied. "The Beasts – Distinguished or otherwise, the Common Peoples, and then we, their Protectors in the absence of the Gods."

"Save for the role of Ascended, I am more unfamiliar with the tiers concerning Amouni society."

"That is also simple enough in order, if not in implementation," the man replied. "All Amouni are, to use a familiar set of terms, Lords and Ladies. Among them, some are blessed with Wings of Ascension, such as yourself."

"And then?"

"Next come Guardians, those Ascended who have made sacrifices in order for more power, and the responsibility that goes with it. This responsibility is usually localised. Some do go on to become Rahnzir, though we are twelve only, to match the Conclave. Eleven now, I suppose," he added.

"And where do Supremes fit into this?"

"During times of peace, they may act as a Guardian would, but during war, they act with Ascended."

"Some Supremes operate between Guardian and Rahnzir," Guardian Min added. "It is not always a clear division."

"Of course, that is true."

Rikeva frowned. "Then where does all of this leave Never?"

"In my estimation, somewhere unsatisfactory – approximately between Guardian and Rahnzir."

Guardian Min narrowed her eyes. "That cannot be confirmed."

"No. But he is Ascended. He not only carries the blood of two Guardians but received the blessing of feathers from the Great Phoenix. More, his knowledge of the future places him above us all, in some ways."

She shook her head. "If you are to fall against the rebels, Rahnzir Sarion, I will maintain control. He may be unique, but he has sworn no Oaths, received no Mandate from the Conclave – he will not act for all Amouni; his chief desire is to leave us."

"Ultimately, that is mine also. But for this task, further study of his blood could settle this."

Guardian Min sighed as she rose to pace before the doorway. "Deeper tests would take too much time. Regular tests to fully understand the memories he holds will still take time. In light of that, what do you propose, Rahnzir Sarion? I cannot refuse your decision, if you wish to make some manner of Field Promotion, as you know, but I believe it will not be necessary."

"Very well. I will merely ask Never a few more questions. However, I would require that you await us outside – at least until I call for your return."

She met his gaze a moment before complying, and again, did not seem pleased.

"The specifics of your discussion are largely lost on me," Never told the Rahnzir. "But I see no reason to place myself above Guardian Min, especially for this task. I only need to convince the Conclave that I am worth assisting."

"Be that as it may, if I can formalise your standing, your voice will be given more weight when you request that which you desire."

"Then ask away," Never replied. "I assume you want to start with the Great Phoenix?"

"Perhaps not. While that is unprecedented in and of itself, I wish to ask about the Blood of the Guardian. Or Guardian*s*."

Time to tread carefully, perhaps. "Specifically?"

"There is something you could not possibly know. Something of which only the Conclave, myself, and my fellow Rahnzir are aware. Something that is yet to grow even into a sapling. Yet you know it will become something magnificent. And you will be there during its demise."

And so he was. "The Memory Tree." Now that the questions were closing in on personal moments of his history, Never found the urge to be less forthcoming push its way to the fore.

"The true name is a somewhat more poetic one. The Evergreen Window. And merely one week prior to this day, it was conceived of by the Conclave. Even then, they envisioned an entire grove. Not a single tree."

Never waited.

"As I'm sure Guardian Min advised, there is no trace of you or your family anywhere. Such things can be achieved… but nor is there a single trace of you having entered even the city where the Conclave meets, let alone their hidden chambers. No trace of their blood, nor the blood of my fellows within you. Only two mysterious Guardians, neither of whom exist today, and thus, neither of which could have stumbled across such a secret in order to tell you."

"Are you asking me to keep that secret?"

He nodded. "And for your companion to do the same."

"Of course," Never replied, Rikeva nodding her agreement. "Wonderful."

"Is that all you wanted to know?"

He smiled now. "I will have more questions about the 'Memory Tree' later. But for now, my final question is about Guardian Ecanseja."

"If you have read my blood, you know that I never met him. Not truly."

"Yes. Perhaps amongst those who are permitted to know what you are, he is of second-most interest. Coming, that is, only after the visions of a future where the Amouni are gone."

"It comes to pass."

He sighed. "Something I am sure we will spend the rest of our lives working to stave off. But returning to Ecanseja, I would prevent the need for his life becoming a Seal against Oleksan."

"Can you?"

"I am not sure. But I will do everything in my power to try. He deserves more."

Never frowned. Was the man actually possessed of a conscience? It was possible, at least. Unlikely, but possible. "Why?"

"He will save the lives of many with his sacrifice. He is a hero, in the true sense of the word. Further, he appears to be my descendant."

Unexpected. "A somehow noble and self-interested reason."

"So it is," Rahnzir Sarion said as he folded his arms. "Now, while your blood speaks, not every detail has been revealed. Not every detail *can* be recovered. But enough exists that I know we must prevent the reawakening of the Burnished King."

Would sharing additional knowledge have unseen consequences? Surely such a ship had already well-and-truly sailed with the tests completed on his blood? Likely, yes. "Then I can say beware, for the Burnished King has two forms. King *and* Queen."

"I see."

"One weakness is marked upon his chest – the Amouni symbol for light. If he rises, strike there, with whatever strong artefact exists in this era."

The man sighed at Never's words and leant back in the chair. "Perhaps that is enough for now." He called for Guardian Min to return.

Never glanced at Rikeva, and it seemed they were both thinking the same thing – the Rahnzir's questions certainly became less an exploration of Never's standing, and more a desire for information.

Equally concerning was the fact that it was no longer possible to guess what the Amouni had already learnt from his blood, and it was always far harder to lie to your enemies when you weren't sure what they already knew.

# Chapter 12.

Once again, they rode by carriage – a somewhat jolting journey while crossing the green plain beyond the city, any echo of the ocean long-since gone. It suggested fewer *forasa* in the Colony, and when Rikeva asked, the Guardian confirmed as much.

"An agreement was reached with Queen Ilekah's ancestors. There are only three on the entire continent."

"Is one not near the site of the tragedy?"

"Yes. But we must first visit the city of Hasollea, which is something of a halfway point. That is where the survivors are being tended to and we must question them. Their conditions are extremely fragile, too fragile to travel."

"What can you tell us about the rebels and the attack?" Never asked. "I think we've all heard enough about me, by now."

"Certainly," she replied. And though the Rahnzir had not settled on any final thoughts regarding Never's standing, it seemed no longer an issue of urgency. Which was troubling in another sense – other, hidden rivalries seemed to be at play. Was it merely a way to needle Guardian Min? She no longer seemed perturbed. "Do you recall that I mentioned their resistance to Amouni gifts?"

"Yes."

"Put very simply, and crudely, they do not burn so easily."

"Well… That is an answer. What else?"

"Most of the rebels come from families and villages that have spent generations close to the site of the tragedy, and it has changed them in other ways. Some are difficult to trace with the naked eye. Even their lesser blood is not always a reliable indicator of their position or movements."

"Lesser blood?"

"You must do your best to accept the terminology used here, Never, if you wish to impress the Conclave."

"Oh, I won't be accepting it. But I can pretend, for their sake."

"A wise decision," Rahnzir Sarion said from his seat, though he did not seem to have his full attention on the conversation.

"Do the Aratho have enough numbers to launch an attack on the capital or the keep? The forces in the north?" Rikeva asked.

"Unlikely," Guardian Min replied. "But our spies *have* recently discovered hints that suggest something deadly is lurking there. Rahnzir Bixuhol's final report mentioned an 'abomination' at the tragedy site; something he believed could be used to destroy a city. It is not clear how the rebels will use it, but we must deal with that threat."

Silence fell across the carriage.

Never frowned. "That sounds significant enough that something ought to have been done sooner. A detail you should have shared before now."

"If it lies within the chasm," Rahnzir Sarion said, his gaze still on the hills of the countryside, "then it will be difficult to reach. Only in the early years do we have reports of people returning from the deep. It will become apparent soon, thanks to you, I am certain."

"At least you are certain," Never said. "I assume the Seeds are what overwhelm those who enter the chasm?"

"They do not help."

Guardian Min continued, "Despite not understanding exactly how the Malecaphera were involved, we know the Seeds can have unpredictable effects on those they meet, those they do not sicken and eventually kill. Somehow, the rebels are using the Seeds against us, and it seems likely they are assisted by whatever is below the earth."

The carriage slowed, then jerked to a halt, cutting off Never's next question. From the driver's seat, the man's voice reached them easily. "There is something you should see, Rahnzir. It's not natural."

Never stepped from the carriage, Rikeva and the Amouni on his heels.

Ahead, a hive-like object rested within the centre of the highway.

Both Guardian and Rahnzir were checking the sky, but Never could not draw his eyes from the hive. It was a thing of elegance, pale yellow curves with what appeared to be shining windows… there was even a pleasant scent, flowers on a spring breeze, unlikely in the heat of summer.

Yet a sense that it was not at all safe was equally strong.

"Turn the carriage around," the Guardian ordered their driver.

Rahnzir Sarion pointed to the sky. "I see them." Pale

wings with a golden tint slipped from his robes, and he leapt to the sky, his fists already searing blue.

"What's happening?" Rikeva asked, staff in hand.

"Flee. Flee north toward Hasollea," the Guardian replied. "We'll hold off the *semir-ko*."

"We can help," Never replied, without taking his gaze from the hive, without even knowing what was inside.

It remained deceptively calm.

"Search your memories and you will know that is not necessarily true." The Guardian had thrown her robe off, revealing a silver breastplate and bare arms covered in runes. "Now, flee! Give the hive wide berth, and do not look back. I can defeat them, but not if I have to protect you both."

Rikeva grabbed his arm. "Never."

He hesitated a moment longer, then ran. From behind, a sweet, almost ethereal voice rose – and he could not be certain of the singer. Guardian or hive? He did not look back. Beside him, Rikeva ran just as hard, her golden curls bouncing.

Only when the song faded completely did they slow, having reached a stone bridge that stretched across a river. It led into a sparse wood of brown and orange leaves that seemed empty enough, definitely no other hives. Never stumbled to a halt halfway across, leaning against the stone rail. Below, clean water ran over uneven rock formations. The river was not fast enough to churn; it left granite-like colours easily visible.

"Can it follow us?" Rikeva asked after catching her own breath. "Or they? Whatever it was."

"I hope not," he replied, glancing back along the road.

"But I should be able to fly again, if we need."

"Let's rest a little longer first."

He nodded.

The hive had seemed to have no specific target, but who had placed it there and why? A trap was likely, especially with Rahnzir Sarion setting off, as if chasing other Amouni? One possibility only. Equally likely, the man sought whatever flying creatures typically lived in the hive.

Had it been the Vadiya?

The rebels ought to have been atop the list. But if so, they hadn't capitalised on getting everyone out of the carriage. That was their perfect moment to launch an attack, and they'd wasted it.

Which suggested a different enemy? A member of the Conclave?

"I haven't seen a map, Never," Rikeva said after a while. "And our provisions are back with the carriage. What do you want to do from here?" Her expression was not one of deep concern, but at her mention of provisions it seemed she held back a wince.

He moved closer. "Do you feel unwell?"

"Yes. But it's nothing I can't handle." She tapped her staff. "I can still fight, so don't worry."

"If you say so."

She smiled. "Hey. I've already told you, no mothering."

He raised both hands. "Sorry."

"So, what about my other questions?"

"Might as well walk while we talk."

She nodded and set off across the bridge. "I'm only too happy to put some space between us and that hive, whatever it was."

"Me too."

"I can't help having mixed feelings about our escorts, however."

Never nodded. Either way, he and Rika were alone now, at least until they reached Hasollea. However long that would take. "Didn't Guardian Min say it was a three-day-ride to Hasollea, back when the carriage first arrived?"

"I think so."

"Then we have a fair journey ahead of us." He glanced around at the trees. They were tall and thin, with fur-laden leaves of brown and orange in spite of the fact that it was not yet autumn. Between the trunks, yellowing grass and the occasional shrub, but no sense of the waterway. "Stupid," he muttered to himself.

"What?"

"We should probably follow the river, or at least turn back and take some water. Maybe we can make flasks… somehow." He shrugged. "I can fly and scout around too. There might be a village that's closer than Hasollea."

She smiled. "The stream's not far, at least."

But when they turned back for the bridge, a figure awaited.

Guardian Min.

Her face was blank, her breastplate gone and her clothing torn – smudges of blood plentiful, but in no danger of soaking through the fabric. The Amouni's eyes were pale pink, pollen seeming to trail the slight movements of her head as she regarded them. Even the woman's wings had been tainted.

And though her mouth moved, no sounds followed.

The only thing that seemed to still be hers were the

runes tattooed into her arms – they were blinking in and out of darkness. As if fighting whatever had come to possess her? Or something more ominous?

She beckoned them near.

# Chapter 13.

He did not take a single step toward the Guardian. Nor did Rikeva, but they were both suddenly standing upon the bridge, snared before they could run.

Pink mist rose from the river, snarling tendrils that clawed for the sky – plentiful enough that the bridge was already lost. Water flowing over rocks became fragmented echoes of the song he'd heard when fleeing the hive. Even the stone at his feet was softening to pink and white. Lines of gold joined the colours, as if he now stood upon quilted petals.

Guardian Min waited before him when he looked up.

He flinched. Only the movement was far too slow when compared to the jolt of shock that ran up his spine. As though the cloying-mist had slowed everything. Petals rose from the floor, closing in and they, too, moved slowly.

Inexorable.

"Never?" Rikeva's voice sounded deeper than it ought.

He called his crimson-fire, and it wavered, as if trapped beneath water. He flung it at the wall of petals with a growl… a futile act. Not only were his arms still painfully slow to move, his movement had 'flung' nothing: the flame merely splashed against the petals and vanished.

"Rikeva?"

She didn't answer. He couldn't see her; the pink fog had thickened. It even concealed Guardian Min and the ever-tightening petals. Already, their horrible softness was pressing his limbs together. His chest was next, air growing thinner.

He had one more trick up his sleeve. Phoenix-flame burst from his hands, from his entire body.

Petals shrivelled, blackening beneath the onslaught.

He kept the flame burning. Harder. Hotter. Steam burst from all around, as if the heat had cut through the bridge to reach the river.

A shriek pierced the air.

Mist began to lift, tarnished petals falling away like a soft sheet. Air returned to his lungs and he stumbled, natural movement restored. Something thumped to the bridge, but a spiralling figure shot into the sky, drawing his gaze.

Guardian Min.

Pink pollen drifted down from where she flew, wings carrying her out of reach.

Rikeva! He spun. She lay upon melted stone. Never knelt, finding the surface cold beneath his knees. He lifted her with an apology; she was still breathing, her eyes fluttering as she regained consciousness.

"We're alive?"

"We are."

She sighed. "What was that?"

"Your guess is as good as mine," he said with a reassuring

smile. "But she's gone."

"Good." She returned his smile, though it was less certain. "Still think you can get us something to drink?"

"Right away." He carried her from the bridge and to the water's edge. There, he set Rikeva down before the earth became too rocky then stepped out into the flow, where he crouched for a moment. How was he going to *bring* her water?

All he really carried were his knives…

And one of Ecanseja's tricks?

Never flipped a blade into his hand, calling the crimson-fire as he did. He let it burn until the steel glowed white, then he pulled the blade into a thinner shape, stretching and moulding it into a tube.

He plunged it into the water. Steam burst free.

Would his creation keep its shape? He was no smith, but hopefully it would hold long enough for Rika to drink. Better if it could last a little while, but then, who knew how close a town or village would be?

After he filled and refilled the thin flask, ensuring it had cooled enough, he was quite pleased that it actually held a modest amount of water. Of most comfort, his blood would have burnt away any lingering impurities after the make-shift forging.

And maybe the blood was what kept it together, too.

He returned and handed her the flask, which she rose to finish in several gulps before thanking him. "Not quite as cold as I'd have liked, but that's impressive, Never."

"We can wait a little while and try again?"

She nodded. "More rest wouldn't hurt. My ribs could be worse, I suppose."

"Mine too." He returned to the river and drank his fill before submerging the tube between some jagged rocks to let it cool further.

"Do you think that could happen again?" Rikeva asked as he returned to sit by her side.

"The Guardian fled, that's all I know for now. Something had definitely possessed her."

"Another threat for us to be wary of, then."

He nodded. "Let me know when you're ready and we'll take a little flight. I think we need to find a village."

"Right." She lay back and closed her eyes. "What about the Rahnzir?"

"No sign yet. I suppose we could try heading back to where we left the carriage and wait. There's no guarantee that the hive is gone."

"It's probably safer to find an inn. The sun must be close to setting."

"True." The sun did hang low in the sky, and while finding a village at night would be easier, his wings would still make the task simple enough, with or without lights on the ground. "You know, I'm quite used to thinking of myself – of the Amouni – as impervious to most threats."

"I probably agree, but aren't we forgetting the Burnished King, for one?"

"Well… yes. But also, not precisely. Oleksan was a god-sized threat. Whatever has possessed Guardian Min is not, in spite of its own power. Something 'lesser' was still enough to trouble me. To trouble us all, including an Amouni with a greater understanding of their own heritage. I don't like it."

She put a hand on his shoulder. "But you still saved us."

"This time. But then… with things like that hive out

there…" He sighed. "And that's not counting whatever is afoot in the wilds or the chasm."

"I can hardly believe what I'm hearing, Never." She was grinning at him.

"What?"

"You, exercising caution."

He chuckled. "I'll try not to make it a habit, My Lady."

She shifted closer, wrapping her arms around him. "I'm sure. But even though I was exaggerating, it wouldn't be a bad idea for us to use that Blood Ward of yours whenever we can."

"Agreed."

"Good. What do you think about taking a flight?"

"Let's find some higher ground."

"Before nightfall."

"Before nightfall, My Lady."

# Chapter 14.

The hill they had found had not been much of one. Still, Never had used it to launch himself and Rikeva into the air. At first, he'd had to claw his way upward until he found some currents to take advantage of, and then it was a more pleasant mixture of gliding and climbing.

Especially as far as his own ribs were concerned.

Woods filled with clearings formed by fallen trunks or campsites alike, rolled by beneath them. While he held a generally northward path, Never circled around whenever the plains opened up for wider stretches, searching for evidence of villages.

Once, a haze of smoke revealed itself to be nothing more than a caravan of wagons who had set up camp early, but the second time he detoured for hints of smoke was a success. Below, a small town was lighting its cook-fires, buildings arranged in an uneven circle around a central square. Fires notwithstanding, he might have caught sight of the rooves without them, since coloured flags flew from the thatching.

"What will we do if they have more rules about the

'Untamed' down there?" Rikeva asked as he circled a clearing. The opening in the trees rested beside a southern road that led into town, and which was empty of travellers.

"I don't know if we have enough of the Amouni coin to bribe them," Never said. He swooped lower, slowing enough to set her down before thudding to the earth himself. "I'd be more than happy to bully the Amouni, but if this village is mostly Arathona folk, then I don't want to resort to that."

"We could try to barter?"

"Let's find out how happy everyone is to see us, then."

They started up the road, soon entering the town. And while he and Rikeva drew their fair share of glances from Arathona in their customary garb, no-one seemed too bothered. People simply attended to their business, returning home with parcels or baskets, or heading toward the market, a place that was still out of sight but which likely waited in the square.

At the first inn, possibly the only one in town, Never stopped. A picture on its sign suggested it was called the Brass Bell, but he could not read the swirling script. And for just a moment, staring up at the sign, a twinge of sadness struck him. One day, perhaps in the distant future – he could not be sure and Ecanseja's memories were of no use – but the people of Arathona, their ribboned clothing, their fanciful script, all of it would be gone. Sunken or destroyed or vanished somehow, and it seemed not even their descendants would survive.

"Is something wrong?" Rikeva asked.

"Nothing." He switched to Marlosi. "It's somehow hard to believe that all of this will be gone one day."

Her expression grew sombre. "And worse, there's probably nothing we can do."

The door swung open and a young woman greeted them. "Are you seeking lodgings, by chance?" Her Amouni was rough, but he understood.

"We are."

"Wonderful." Her gaze moved to Rikeva, then back to Never. "There's a small problem, Davischa."

"No need for formalities. Tell us the problem?"

"Well, we offer only single rooms," she said, then glanced briefly to the sky. "As Idilor would will it."

"Ah…"

"What I mean, My Lord, is that the rooms are for one person only, you see. Most Amouni have no issue with this custom."

He reached for the purse. "We may have enough for two rooms."

"Forgive me, but only one room remains." She lowered her voice. "There is also only one inn here in Netaal."

He waved a hand. "No need to apologise." Yet it was a problem.

The young woman bowed her head. "You could fly to Hasollea, though it would take most of the night, I imagine."

"Please, we are not angry," Rikeva said. "Has the innkeeper ever made exceptions to this rule?"

Her eyes widened. "Oh, I don't know if I could ask Reanlo that…"

"We can," Never assured her. "If you wouldn't mind introducing us?"

She took them inside, passing through a quiet common room with wooden tables and a banked but unlit fire, and to the bench. There, an older man with something of a pinched face waited.

"Welcome to the Brass Bell," the innkeeper said with a smile. "Seeking rooms or only a meal, perhaps, My Lord?"

"Actually, we hoped to ask about your single-room custom."

He nodded, motioning to the young woman. "Kalo, would you mind lending a hand in the kitchen, dear?"

"Certainly." She set off down a dim hallway.

He moved around the counter. "Forgive me for saying, Davischa, but despite your wings, you don't wholly resemble other Amouni…"

Never smiled. "I appreciate the compliment. I can offer fire as proof, if you wish?"

"Just a lick of flame in your hand, if that isn't too much trouble."

He called the crimson-fire, letting it dance for just a moment. "As you can see, I am as I claim."

"So you are," the innkeeper said with a nod, though concern was evident upon his face.

Rikeva smiled. "We don't wish to trample across your customs, but we are weary from travel. Maybe there's a problem we could solve, especially given Never's Amouni gifts?"

"Well… Now that you offer, some weeks back we put in a request for aid to both the royal guard and the Rahnzir's people. Unanswered, so far, I'll add." Reanlo lowered his voice. "If you could help the town, I'd be willing to make an exception this night."

"Tell us more," Never said.

"Something has been spooking the animals for some

time now. Supposedly, it's happening over at Tirle, too." He shook his head. "At first, we thought it was just wolves. Or maybe even a bear come down from the mountains in the west. But old Erda's place is quite close to the cave that we think is actually the source of the problem."

"You've investigated?"

"We did. We found… pieces of cattle, and plenty of bloody feathers leading inside. Thought we had our answer. And I suppose we did, but *something* took Henl, and the rest of us fled. We haven't seen Henl since and no-one knows what's in there. When I was a lad, it was just a cave with a pool at the back, nothing else."

"And was Henl the only one to disappear?"

"No-one else dared head inside. Animals still disappear, but less frequently now that we've moved some of the pens," Reanlo explained. "But who knows if the creature will change its mind and start looking for food here?"

"Worry not. We'll deal with whatever it is tomorrow," Never said.

The man's eyes brightened. "Thank you, Davischa!"

"Simple provisions enough to reach Hasollea wouldn't go astray, either."

"It would be my pleasure. And for this evening?"

"Whatever you have."

"Just milk for me," Rikeva added.

"Of course, My Lady. Let me show you to your room first." He took them down a corridor opposite the kitchen and opened the final door, lit by a setting sun that slipped through a curious window: constructed of six rectangular slots running down the wall, rather than a single pane of glass. "I'll return with your meals and the key," he added, pushing the door open with a smile then rushing off.

Inside, Never found a narrow room with a single bed, chair and writing desk against the wall. A chest had been tucked beneath the desk and a small window admitted more orange light. "The girl wasn't joking about the size of the rooms."

Rikeva took the chair. "Or the bed. We won't both fit."

"I can take the floor," he said as he closed the door. "There's something else worrying me."

"The cave?" she asked. "It can't be worse than whatever happened to Guardian Min."

"A mere beast *would* be a welcome change. But I mean you, Rikeva. What's happening with your appetite?"

She sighed. "It's the food here. I can barely keep it down. You didn't hear me throwing up back in the city?"

"No... I must have been focused on the Blood Ward," he replied. "I'm sorry. I hadn't realised it was quite this bad."

"It might not be. I mean, I don't feel as though I'm being poisoned. But even if I *do* manage to keep something down, it wreaks havoc on my stomach. Liquids aren't much better."

He sat upon the bed with a frown. Poisoning on behalf of the Amouni was unlikely, especially since so many of them seemed to want his help. Nor, for that matter, poisoning by anyone else. It also seemed unlikely that she was reacting to Amouni magic, like use of the *forasa*, since she'd travelled via the symbols plenty of times before. It was something simpler – the food itself, as Rikeva suspected.

Yet why? The food was hardly reserved for Amouni only, since other peoples had the same diet... other peoples who had been doing so all their lives.

Of course.

"You aren't used to food from this era, and why would you be? Whereas I am Amouni, so I've been able to adjust."

She nodded slowly. "Is this something the Amouni will have to solve?"

"Their healers probably could, if we wait to find one," he said. "But you have my blood now – if you want to use it."

"Better than relying on the Amouni, I think."

"I'm happy to try if you are, but it changes people, remember?"

"Usually for the better, from what you've told me."

"I hope that's true."

She smiled. "It is. Let's see some blood, Never."

# Chapter 15.

He laughed. "Sounds like you're looking forward to it."

She offered a slight shrug in response. "You've mentioned it before. For Sascha and Mukatagami, and they're both fine."

"It improved their healing and probably extended their life spans. Other than that, I'm not certain what else could happen. To them or you."

She crossed her legs at the ankle. "We might not have a lot of other options."

"Well, aside from finding an Amouni healer in Hasollea, we could wait to see whether you adjust to the food here on your own?"

"Assuming I trust the Amouni."

"Yes."

"Which I don't."

"Yes."

"Well, I trust *you*, so let's see what happens with your blood. I'm getting too hungry to wait much longer."

"If you're certain."

"I am."

"Keep in mind that I don't know if it will work at all," he said. "Or how long it might take to work, and if it does –"

"Never. So be it."

A knock upon the door followed her words, and Never admitted Kalo, the young woman from earlier. She held a wooden tray with steaming soup, bread and roasted potatoes bearing some manner of herb-crust. A mug of ale sat beside one of milk, which Rikeva took once the woman set the tray down.

"I hope you will be comfortable here," she said with a nod. "I apologise for the narrow range of options – it's a little early in the evening, and so this is mostly left-over from the midday meal."

"Not a problem," Never said around a mouthful of bread. "Actually, if you had some extra blankets or a bedroll for the floor?"

"Of course, I'll get that right away."

Once the woman had returned with blankets, apologising yet again from the doorway as she left, Never rested the bundle on the table and drew his knife. He knelt beside Rikeva, who still held her milk. "Ready?"

"I am."

He sliced through the skin of his palm and let blood run down his fingers to drip into the milk. No more than a dozen drops, as he had no idea how to estimate what would be enough.

"Let me know if it improves the flavour of the milk," he said.

Rikeva laughed. "I'm not expecting it to, to be honest." She lifted the cup and drank without pause.

"Well?"

"There's a tang that is not entirely the fault of the milk," she said once she'd finished, then set the mug down with a shrug. "Now we wait."

Never started on the meal, making certain to save her some bread, though she did not feel confident to try more food so soon. And so he melted another spoon for a Blood Ward, then they sought their rest, having made only minimal plans for the morrow.

Too much was unknown, and so there was little to do but wait for the dawn. Certainly after the attack, after flying with still-healing ribs, after creating the Blood Ward too, Never was weary enough that he had no trouble falling asleep, even on the hard floor.

In the morning, Rikeva assured him she was fine and so they rose and prepared to leave swiftly.

Downstairs, a man in a tunic and pants that bore no ribbons met them in the common room, now quite busy as travellers and locals ate at the tables. None were Amouni, a fact Never was uncertain how to interpret. While the fellow wore a scarf of faded blue, unlike other locals, he also wore a hat with a wide brim, white hair peeking from beneath. "Reanlo asked me to show you the cave, if you're ready, Davischa?" Like all they'd encountered in Aratho, the man spoke Amouni with an accent.

"We are, but you can call me Never. I'm not much one for titles."

"Ah... yes. Well, of course, My Lord," he said, clearly unsure of how to respond. "My name is Erda, and my farm is one that borders the hills where the cave is, but I suppose you know that much already."

"How far?" Rikeva asked with a nod.

"A short walk to the western field. Just out of town, really."

"Then lead on," Never told the man.

The streets were far busier than what he'd found in the Amouni city, with other farmhands bringing food toward the market, or children in much plainer clothing chasing one another or their pet dogs – and just as often, helping their elders.

Similar to the previous evening, few people seemed troubled by Never, and certainly not Rikeva, allowing an easy passage to the edge of town and then into the fields where a soft breeze stirred the grass.

Their guide climbed a low wooden fence and pointed. "It's been fair quiet the last week, but that might not be a good sign." He gestured then to the neighbouring field, where cattle huddled together by the fence nearest to a farmhouse and barn. A few grunts from the animals crossed the grass. "As you can see, the cows don't much want to be alone."

Never nodded, letting his gaze roam to the aforementioned hills. A stand of thin trees grew beside an opening that bore the look of a deep slash, its shadows impenetrable. Temporary fencing blocked the trail that led to the cave, but the cave-mouth itself was clear. "Has anyone seen the creature?"

"Only Henl, sadly. From the remains after those first attacks, we think its claws and teeth are plenty large. Bigger than any wolf."

"And not a bear?"

The man scratched at stubble on his cheek. "It doesn't seem to be, no."

"We'll let you know what we find," Never said. He called

twin globes of crimson-fire. "Or burn, I suppose."

He led Rikeva across the field and around the temporary fence where he paused. No hint of movement or sound from within. He shrugged as he entered. His fire lit uneven walls, casting them in an unpleasant colour that brought the Red Seed Cult to mind.

But no monstrous animal was revealed. Only bones and scraps of feathers.

"How deep?" Rikeva asked.

He flared the light, and a twist appeared in the cave passage. "At least a little farther."

But they'd barely taken half a dozen steps down the new direction when a growling reached Never – the source revealed only when the cavern opened up.

Something fur-covered rose from a small pool of water.

Its many eyes gleamed under the crimson-fire, four heavy arms splashing free. Talons gleamed on each limb. Never only caught a glimpse of the face – a wide jaw lined with fangs – then he lanced it with twin beams of searing flame.

The thing collapsed with a roar, writhing in place, steam bursting from the pool.

Never kept the fire burning until the creature stopped moving.

A hot, pungent scent filled the cavern, enough that he grimaced. "I hope that was the only one."

"The cave doesn't go any deeper, so you're probably right," Rikeva said.

He turned to leave but did not take a single step.

Guardian Min blocked the exit.

A faint pink glow deepened where it met light from the

crimson-fire. She appeared as before, though the blood was now dried. Her eyes were still blank, and pollen still drifted when she moved, this time to take a single step forward.

"Help me."

# Chapter 16.

Never did not let the crimson-fire fade as he raised his voice. "Guardian, can you hear me?"

She did not answer. Her body trembled, as though she fought from within. Pollen fell free from around her face as she strove to speak again, as best he could tell. When she lifted an arm, petals drifted to the damp stone.

"Never, her hand."

It was not holding petals – it was *made* of petals.

"How do we help you?" Never shouted.

The Guardian spun, fleeing the cave. He gave chase but by the time he burst free, Rikeva on his heels, the Amouni had already taken to the skies – flying faster than he'd ever seen. Petals and pollen fluttered in the air where she'd been mere heartbeats ago.

"I don't know if I could catch her," he said, frowning up at the dark clouds gathered in the sky.

"Even if you could, what would you do?" Rikeva asked. She bent to pick up a few petals, frowning at the soft pink.

"This is not wholly like a true plant, that much I can tell."

"Are you sure they're safe to touch?"

"No. But if you think we need the Guardian, and she appears again, maybe I can figure something out. I'm not a stranger to plant-life, at least."

He nodded. "This may sound strange, but more than the Supreme or Rahnzir, I believe we might be able to trust the Guardian a little more."

"Probably." She added the petals to her coin pouch, then wiped her hands upon her clothing.

Footsteps approached; Erda, running across the field.

His eyes were wide when he arrived. "You're alive!"

"We are."

"Then you got whatever it was – even with the Sleeping Fairy, right?"

Sleeping Fairy? Was that a translation of *semir-ko*? "A furred creature with four arms," Never said. "Dead now. What do you mean by Sleeping Fairy?"

"You drove her off somehow," the farmer continued, and now his expression changed to one of admiration. "Usually it takes two or three of you lot, as I understand it."

A concerning revelation. "What else do you know about these Sleeping Fairies?"

Rikeva added a question of her own. "Is she likely to return?"

The man removed his hat to scratch at his head. "Couldn't say. I've only ever seen one around these parts. Must have been at least forty years ago now. They prefer the islands to the west."

"And they possess and then change people?"

"They do," he said. "But I couldn't explain it. You'd need

to ask someone up in Hasollea, for that. In their Hall of Learning. Good folk there, too. Whenever they come, it's with new ideas about how to get a better yield out of the land. Might be worth a visit."

"We'll do just that," Never replied.

He thanked the man and set off for the northern road with Rikeva at this side. Her staff was still held ready and her gaze roved the sky above the trees.

No sign of the Guardian, the Rahnzir or any other Amouni flying across all the grey.

Not on the road either, which was well-maintained with carefully fitted stone, gutters and grooves for stormwater to run off. In fact, not even locals or travelling Arathona were using the highway. A hush had fallen over the wood, even as it thinned, and more sounds ought to have reached them.

But not even a bird.

Not even the crack of thunder overhead.

"What now?" Rikeva asked after a time. "It could be the weather, but this doesn't seem natural."

"Just a moment of quiet in an isolated part of Aratho?"

"I think we should cover a bit of ground." She slipped her staff between the loops of her pack. "Do you feel up to another flight?"

"North it is, then," he said with a nod, and this time it was a little easier to take to the skies. Were his wings stronger? Maybe they'd needed warming up after a period of disuse, prior to yesterday's flight.

The forest below soon became a marshland of grey water and yellowing shrubs, stretching as far as he could see in all directions. The road wove throughout but was now supported by regular bridges of varying sizes. Mostly stone, some were also constructed with silvery ropes, gleaming as if independent from the absent sun.

And despite regular stops to give his and Rikeva's grip some respite, a longer pause was in order by noon, when he landed on what was obviously a common campsite. It had been built around a large fire-pit, protected by modest stone walls that reached only chest-height. It was sturdy enough and would provide at least some shelter.

Benches surrounded the fire-pit but were spread around points farthest from the nearby road, something less common. Four sets of rectangular pods built from quartz had been set into the stone, complete with carved instructions explaining how Ascended Amouni could arrange their wings, once inside.

"Reminds me of clear coffins," Rikeva said when they stood before them. "Like the one from our Temple Trivium."

A voice called a greeting from the sky.

An Amouni with dark wings approached, robes fluttering as he circled lower. He wore a thin beard and a bright smile as he landed to approach. "Greetings, travellers. Are you heading toward Hasollea, by chance?"

"We are, yes," Never replied.

"If you are yet to seek your rest, I'd be more than happy to share some news while I take a meal," he added as he settled onto a bench. There, he removed soft bread covered in spices, and began to eat. "I am Votejoma, before I forget. Ascended, and little else," he added with a wink.

Encouraged by the man's uncommonly friendly nature, Never introduced himself as Ascended, and Rikeva as Quisoan. "Is something amiss in Hasollea?"

He smiled at both Never and Rikeva. "Increased rebel scheming. Especially after Rahnzir's death. I assume you're aware?"

"We are."

Votejoma took another few bites. "Stay wary, then."

"Are you expecting an attack on Hasollea?" Rikeva asked.

"It's hard to judge. Whatever is happening farther north is the main concern, of course. Has been for a long time." He finished his bread and stood. "Well, I have news to deliver. One other thing I can recommend when you arrive, is to have your Seed Collar ready. There's been a dark wind, of late."

"We appreciate the warning," Never said as the man took a running leap from the edge of the stone wall, a single feather falling free as he headed for the sky. How refreshing to meet an Amouni who was not insufferable. Or full of prejudice.

But there was a problem.

Never shook his head as he turned from the sky. "Our collars are back in the carriage, aren't they?"

"I shouldn't be surprised," Rikeva said. "Considering our luck so far – but I am."

"If we come across a village before Hasollea, we might be able to find one. Or buy one, once we're inside the city," he said.

"If nothing else, we can use those scarf-masks the Aratho wear."

"Perfect." He took a seat on the nearest bench, unslung his pack and began to sift through whatever the innkeeper had provided. "Think you can keep something down, today?"

She'd already joined him, one arm deep in her own pack. "I do."

# Chapter 17.

And she had, much to Never's relief.

And her own.

Especially considering that when they arrived before Hasollea's walls as night fell, Rikeva was still yet to feel any ill-effects from an unsettled stomach.

In spite of his relief, a wave of weariness had him dragging his feet a little as they approached the city. Hasollea's walls gleamed in the lamplight; a mix of granite and quartz —each construction-material arranged in mighty, alternating columns. It was a marvel, and through enormous steel gates that stood open, Never spied similar buildings inside, though all on a much more modest scale.

Even with smaller amounts of quartz being used, it allowed an interesting range of shades to be refracted – especially with coloured lamps in place. One street appeared mostly blue while yellow poured from the edge of a nearby square.

Yet more noteworthy might have been the mix of Amouni and royal guards that lined the walls. The Aratho were armed with bows, as were the Amouni – and their arrows were faintly blue.

All wore either mask or collar.

At the gate, Never stopped before a pair of Guides. The Amouni servants had been joined by Royal Aratho soldiers in their green and black armour, these also carrying swords. Without seeming to confer, all four figures urged them into the city with either nods or waves.

"Where could we find the Rahnzir?" Never asked before entering. "And masks."

*Rahnzir Sarion is in the Infirmary, Master. He is not accepting petitioners until tomorrow.*

"And the location of the infirmary?"

*The centre of the city.*

He looked to one of the Aratho. "What of the masks?"

"Most merchants sell them," the man replied, then shrugged. "If you don't mind a short wait, we have several spare."

"That would be most welcome."

The soldier stepped into the nearby guardhouse, which had been built into the very wall, and soon returned with the scarf-masks and their resin eye-holes. He offered a quick demonstration before handing them over, Rikeva thanking him as they set off.

The nearer they came to the city-centre, the busier the cobbled streets grew, with Aratho and Amouni alike moving about, talking, shouting, trading – much more like a proper city. And while he was pleased to note there was no sign of any Seed attacks, since few people seemed to be wearing their scarves as masks yet, he *was* growing weary of so many coloured lights.

No single building or street boasted too much, no street or building was completely stained by the reflected lights either, but it was with a small sigh when he and Rikeva found themselves standing before the Infirmary.

Built of white stone or steel, not unlike the Temples, this building had been lit by pale light. The place was something of a beacon, standing several storeys tall. Had he looked down on it from above, its vague cross-shape would probably appeared clearer still. Each point bore a quartz entryway, and even as they paused, a pair of Amouni carried an Aratho child inside at a run.

"How do we find Rahnzir Sarion in there?" Rikeva asked.

"Hopefully a Guide," he said as he started for the nearest entry.

No sooner had they set foot inside a broad reception area with long corridors and quartz shafts, than the Rahnzir stepped from one of them with a nod.

An Amouni who'd risen from a nearby desk, as if to question them, retook his seat at the Rahnzir's entrance.

"It is pleasing to see you survived, Never," the man said. He did not greet Rikeva.

"More evidence for your classification?" he asked.

"In part."

"What of Guardian Min? Do you know who attacked us and why?"

He gestured back to the quartz shaft from which he'd only just stepped. "Join me on the roof and I will share what I know, and what I believe must now be done."

"You learnt something from the survivors?" Rikeva asked once the quartz… box began to rise. And as she spoke, she faced the Amouni with her whole body rather than simply turning her head, as if to force him to acknowledge her.

"Enough to know that whatever it is down there is fast becoming every bit the threat Rahnzir Bixuhol believed it was. I now suspect the Conclave had long been dismissive of his concerns."

The quartz slowed, soon coming to a halt.

Outside, the rooftop was dim but the Amouni led them toward a balcony where light from the streets below illuminated the rail. It also shone on several large silver… constructions. Slings with handrails?

"For swift departure, if needed," the Amouni said when he noticed Never examining one.

Rikeva glanced around. "Are we speaking here because you don't trust the healers?"

"No. But there may be others within the halls that we would do well to be wary of."

"Rebels or Amouni?"

"Possibly both. But my concern is reserved for whoever organised the attack on our carriage. I could not catch them, but I suspect they have come to Hasollea."

Never leant against the sling. "Who was responsible?"

"I have no name. But invariably, it will be someone linked to the Conclave, with several candidates among those that disagree with our plans – and with your survival, of course."

Nothing new, in a way. "Then we should set our own trap."

Rahnzir Sarion smiled. "I appreciate that you are willing to fight back."

"Can we? Now that we are without Guardian Min? You said you could explain."

"That was… unfortunate," he said, sounding somewhat insincere. "From what I have discovered, she is lost. There is no point trying to save her; she will only destroy you too, Never."

"She spoke to us," he replied with a frown.

The man paused, only to shrug. "And what of her eyes and her hands?"

"Of pollen. Petals fell to the ground when she lifted her hands."

"Then she cannot be saved. The *semir-ko* has replaced her mind. In time, she will become another hive, like that which was set during the trap. Guardians will be dispatched to destroy her before such a thing occurs."

Was the man telling the truth about her fate? Too difficult to say. His attitude could have been utterly typical Amouni, or it could have revealed more evidence of a power struggle or pre-existing rivalry.

It may also have been the truth. The man could merely have wanted to focus on the problem at hand. Even so, Never could not shake a lingering doubt about the Rahnzir's words.

Above all, Guardian Min defended them.

Rikeva had folded her arms. "Are we likely to face another hive?"

"I cannot say, but I doubt we will. They rarely survive travelling the distance from their home, and even then, they pose a significant risk to those who would use them as a weapon."

"Pointing to a member of the Conclave, as you suspect."

"Yes. But ferreting out that secret must wait a little longer, at least. I want you both well-rested before tomorrow."

"Hard to do with a dagger in my chest," Never replied.

"You will be safe in the Temple. In any event, I am not expecting a fresh attack now that the first one failed. I believe it more likely to come when we are at our most vulnerable; engaged with the rebel force on the morrow, or exploring the chasm."

His reasoning was sound enough. "Where will we meet, then?"

"There is a *forasa* gate north of the city. I have ordered our forces to gather there shortly after dawn, and will join you once I have attended to matters left unfinished by my predecessor."

Never nodded. "Very well."

# Chapter 18.

At the Infirmary's exit, Never found their path blocked by a pair of Amouni. Their robes featured symbols of trees upon their chests, the so-called Alleviators? They were wheeling something quite familiar inside – a man of silver, crafted with vague features only.

Awfully similar to the artefact that rested within Pacela's Spire, which Ecanseja had recognised as a Diving Skin… yet was this different? The man's memory wasn't helping. If so, what purpose would healers have for such an item?

Never asked for a moment of their time. "Can I inquire as to the purpose of this?"

One of the Amouni, the younger woman of the two, smiled. "Oh, are you interested in the healing arts?"

"Specifically this marvellous creation," Never said.

"Well, as much as I would agree with you, they are not as popular as we'd have hoped," she replied.

"Oh?"

"Few are willing to take the risk," the other woman added.

"Which, I suppose is fair," the younger replied with a sigh. "They're not true solutions, after all."

Never glanced from face-to-face. "Risks? For diving?"

The older Amouni frowned. "I'm not sure what you mean. There was something like that being researched, but after the difficulties with the Liquid Armour, I don't really know where it stalled."

"Then this is for healing?"

"Very much. In this case, we are hoping to save one of the victims of the Seed attack, where the Shade was involved."

"I see."

"They have agreed to enter the Silver Skin and sleep until we are better able to heal their affliction," she said. "And speaking of which, we'd best continue our work."

"Of course." Never stepped aside. The silver man was nothing that would help them now… though it raised the question of exactly what waited back in Pacela's Spire.

"Let's keep moving," Rikeva said. "We don't know if we're being watched, remember?"

He nodded, and set off for the Temple at a brisk walk, despite a creeping weariness. Once they reached the pale building, being admitted without challenge and shown to a simple room with typically pale walls, Never summoned strength from somewhere and used it to seal them in before finally collapsing onto one of the beds.

"No plans to eat, then?" Rikeva asked from where she was rummaging through their pack.

"I'll eat two breakfasts," he murmured, and then the softness of sleep closed in.

***

In the city's north, quartz in most buildings appeared far less ostentatious; a mere brightness, especially considering the muted light from above. Despite the early hour, Never felt no lingering sleepiness – the day ahead was too important.

While there hadn't been food enough for a second breakfast, what he'd eaten was enough. Rikeva, too, was still able to keep her meals down.

"Are you sure about this, Never?" Rikeva asked as she detoured a local man, the fellow having stopped in the street to remove something from one of his boots.

He grinned. "Aside from all the doubts, you mean?"

"I do."

"Well, I trust Rahnzir Sarion less than ever."

"Exactly. He was definitely hiding something about the *semir-ko*," she said. "If I had a little more time, I might have learnt something to help. We could still visit that Hall of Learning first. Or go back to the Infirmary. The Rahnzir would simply have to wait."

She'd examined the petals over breakfast while they discussed exactly how important saving Guardian Min might be, and whether she could be a true ally, along with the Rahnzir's hidden motives – only to come up empty-handed on all fronts.

Equally, they learnt little about the Seeds, finding few answers amongst the Temple inhabitants. The Seeds grew – and flew – chiefly from the site of the tragedy, where whatever had fallen from the sky destroyed half a forest.

But no-one truly knew what they were.

Which was the whole problem the Amouni and Artho were trying to solve.

Rikeva had been just as uncertain about their path – concerns he definitely shared. Even so, the best they'd come up with – if the Rahnzir did have betrayal in his heart – was attempting to take the *forasa* Gate by force then escaping to Kiymako.

Immediately ensuring they would be hunted…

Another world of uncertainties.

"He would have to wait for us," Never agreed. "And honestly, that would probably please a petty part of me."

"But?"

He came to a halt, allowing a group of royal soldiers astride horses to pass. They rode from the direction of celebrations before a large tavern, if the crowds, flags and lively music were an accurate indication. But before he could answer Rikeva, a Guide's face flickered into view beneath a nearby lamp – once more, their features the same as those he and Snow had once fought.

Bells chimed too, and the Guide spoke. *Subjects and Common Peoples. A Seed Storm is inbound today. Please prepare accordingly.*

The Guide repeated the warning twice more then vanished.

Rikeva frowned. "How long do you think we have?"

Never glanced around. No-one was in a state of panic, let alone in a rush to protect themselves, they merely continued about their tasks. Would there be a second warning, closer to the arrival of the Seeds? "A little time, by the looks of things." They continued on. "I've forgotten what I was meaning to say."

"About the Hall of Learning or the Infirmary."

"Right. If there *is* a trap, set by the Rahnzir or anyone else, they'll know that's our most logical step."

"That's only true if whoever is behind the attack believes we actually trust Guardian Min enough to try saving her. There might not be a trap at either location, and there could just as easily be a trap anywhere else."

He nodded. "And no escort to take us to the gate this morning. Are we being exposed to threats on purpose?"

"More testing by the Rahnzir?"

Despite Never's doubts, he did not feel any more danger than usual. And yet… "I'm not enjoying all this second guessing. We did enough before."

She sighed. "Me either."

"Then let's put a stop to this city-destroying threat as planned. We return as heroes – or at least return with everyone indebted to us, and hope that's a better chance of staying alive long enough to help Guardian Min before we leave."

"Can she wait that long?"

He'd asked himself the same question. Because saving even a potential enemy from such a horrific fate was likely the right thing to do. At the very least, *trying*. And she'd asked for help; she wasn't lost. "I don't know."

"Let's press Rahnzir Sarion for more information. Maybe Guardian Min *can* survive longer than we think."

He nodded; it would have to be enough.

Because in the end, a choice between saving the woman and whatever had to be done in order to return home, would mean that Guardian Min was doomed. Unless she could somehow recover on her own.

When they reached the dark arch with its *forasa* symbol, it stood within a broad, stone courtyard ringed by what seemed to be the city barracks, a place where quartz was in short supply. Regular, narrow windows still held a few lights, but most of the inhabitants seemed ready to depart.

Arathona soldiers wore leather armour and despite the Seed Storm warning, for now at least, their scarves hung around their necks.

The Amouni were more uniform in their fine robes and occasional belt knife. Equally so when it came to their faces, which were mostly quite regular or fine of feature. But seeing a large number together for the first time, a little more variety *was* present in the Amouni; their bodies ranging from stout to slender, short to tall.

It was something of a surprise, having met only the 'elite' among them so far – an elite whose most discernible differences tended to be the colour of their wings.

No-one smiled or even greeted them. Some whispered, and others wore rather hostile expressions.

One man actually made a hand gesture that was presumably obscene.

Never grinned back.

"Sarion seems to be dawdling," Rikeva said after a time. She leant against her staff, frowning at the Amouni.

Before Never could respond, one of the Ascended broke from the ranks to approach. He was slender, and his hair gleamed even in the modest post-dawn light. "You are the mongrel, aren't you? If not, you certainly look the part. Clear Marlosi taint, if I'm not mistaken."

Never raised an eyebrow. Said nothing.

"Do you even understand me?" the man asked with a deep frown.

Still, he did not speak, certain now that he had chosen the correct method to antagonise the fop.

"Do not play dumb. You are foul. A mutt. And no matter what the Rahnzir claims, you will not be recognised as anything else."

He spun to stride back toward his fellows.

So be it.

Never removed a coloured Amouni coin – the larger denomination in green – and hurled it at the back of the man's head.

# Chapter 19.

The Amouni pitched forward, reaching for his head as he spun. His dark eyes were wild with outrage, and an expectant hush had fallen over the crowd.

Almost too easy to provoke.

Though for their own part, the royal soldiers who watched seemed quite pleased.

"Never, is this a good idea?" Rikeva asked, speaking in Quisoan as the Amouni bent, searching for the coin.

He nodded. "It occurred to me that now is a good a time as any to prove myself."

"Assuming they were ever going to cooperate properly."

"Assuming that, yes."

The Amouni had finally snatched up the coin, and now he stormed forward. "What is the meaning of this pathetic infraction?" Spittle flew from his mouth as he spoke. "I demand a reckoning! You will face me now, in a duel, with all gathered as witness to the outcome."

"Hmmm. Isn't a duel fought over matters of honour?"

"Of course, fool!"

"Then I cannot accept – after all, only one of us has any."

The Amouni fellow began to tremble. Sapphire-flames burst from his hands, but two of his fellows rushed forward, each taking a shoulder. "Udali, wait. If you want to do this, do it properly."

"He isn't worth it," the other one said, her own expression one of distaste. Her hair was a pale, pale blonde and her cheeks seemed to have been graced with a touch of soft pink.

Never shrugged. "I don't mind teaching all three of you some manners – if you're not too afraid, of course."

"What?" The Amouni who'd spoken first was blinking, his eyes holding more shock.

Once again, Never could not help but notice just how easy they were to enrage – so utterly unaccustomed to being challenged.

Especially by those they felt lesser.

Udali's flames eased and he seemed to calm himself somewhat. "You cannot be serious."

"I know you heard me." Never raised his voice then, gesturing to the open square. "Now, do something about it, you pompous little insects."

"Fine. You will face us all."

The pale woman shrugged but did not leave, and the man was nodding beside Udali.

"I must object, My Lords and Ladies." One of the Arathona approached. An older man with grey at his temples, his expression bearing a trace of weariness. "No result of such a single-sided contest will count for honour, and we are awaiting the new Rahnzir. He would not approve, I am certain."

Udali waved the man away. "Return to your post, Captain."

"Very well." He rejoined his men, who still seemed to be quite invested in the outcome.

"What are the conditions for our bout?" Never asked.

"Obviously, we will skip language, music and art," Udali said. "We will focus solely on arms – all gifts, but no weapons." He glanced at his fellows, who both nodded.

"And how will I know that you have yielded?" Never asked. "First blood is obviously of no use."

The man shook his head. "You are arrogant for a mongrel to assume you have any chance of victory."

"Simply by word," the woman replied.

"Allow me to set aside a few knives," he said, and moved to Rikeva, handing over the first two from his belt.

"Do you still think this is a good idea?" she asked.

He passed her a third dagger. "Ask me after I prevail."

"Never."

On his final dagger, Rikeva caught his hand. "What do I do if you've misjudged this fight?"

"Try to find Rahnzir Sarion." He added his cloak. "It shouldn't be hard. I suspect he'll be watching this."

"Are you sure of that?"

"Not truly."

She stomped on his foot, not too hard. "Then you'd better win."

Never smiled then strode to the centre of the square. Murmurs of anticipation rose, the crowd seeming to lean in. His opponents were already spreading into a triangle, hands ablaze. Two bore red crimson-fire, but Udali's flame was blue once more, like the Rahnzir.

No matter, since it wasn't hotter than Phoenix fire.

And based on his few encounters when it came to flame-against-flame, willpower counted for much when it came to overcoming an opponent, as much as actually feeling the heat.

That, and surprises.

Even so, he was facing three Amouni at once.

The Amouni each let their wings free – white, white, and black. But he did not follow suit. Instead, he called his own fire and charged the dark-eyed man. If nothing else, it would likely insult Udali, who no doubt saw himself as the most important.

His enemy skipped backward, hurling fire.

Never dodged, then rolled before the woman's attack could land, flames splashing across the stone.

And when he found his feet, it was to come face-to-face with Udali and his blue fire.

Yet, he'd hoped as much.

Never flared his crimson flame enough to protect his entire body and swung his first punch. The man blocked and purple flames sprayed, but Never wove around to smash his birch hand into the man's ribs.

The Amouni stumbled to one knee, blue flame vanishing as he gasped for air.

Shouts of anger were enough of a warning for Never to skip back, as yet more fire scorched the stone. Despite their failed attack, the other Amouni were still closing in; the woman swooping down from above and the man thundering across the ground.

Never cut his flame and switched to blood only – letting it spray forth.

Both opponents faltered.

As expected. The fools thought it impure; the woman tilting her wings and the man flaring his own fire as dark blood splashed.

Never pounced, his fist cracking into the man's jaw before the blood had even finished hissing. The Amouni fell back. He raised his own fists to protect his face – a little too high, since it obscured his view.

Perfect. Never already had a new target – he caught one wing in both hands and wrenched them together.

Bone snapped.

A scream shot through the square. Cries of horror echoed from the gathered Amouni, barely audible over the blood pumping in Never's ears. He shoved the Amouni to one side – the woman was somewhere behind him, and Udali had not yet risen.

But the Amouni was up to something… The fop had pressed his palms upon the ground, blue fire swirling.

And then it vanished.

Only to burst up before Never! Bars of blue flame trapped him. He flared his own crimson-fire just as the woman attacked.

She'd landed nearby, fire bursting forth.

The man rose too, his twisted face a picture of agony, but not enough to stop him adding his own flame to the torrent. Heat began to slip beneath Never's defences, enough to drive him to his own knees.

But he was hardly finished.

Never flared the Phoenix's flame and reached out to swipe through the bars – only for each one to snap back into place.

Udali limped forward. "Yield or die, filth."

# Chapter 20.

Crimson and sapphire clashed – the colours surviving amongst a purple storm fierce enough to take his breath away. His whole body screamed for relief as the Holy Fire struggled to hold off the concentrated effort of three Amouni.

Someone might have been calling his name, but all he could hear for certain was the crackle of flames. Worse, the scent of his skin beginning to burn had reached him.

Pain grew. It was already too much!

His body trembled. Agony overwhelmed him, leaving his mind almost blank – leaving nothing but the urge to lash out blindly.

New flames roared.

A bloody film covered Never's vision.

He saw enough to know that the cage was gone yet the Amouni had not given up. They continued to pour their flame upon him. The woman's eyes seemed wide with horror, the man was shouting for him to yield, and Udali was smiling; an expression of such joy that Never's stomach flipped.

Somewhere deep within, hidden inside his blood, a speck of darkness stirred.

His jaw was clenched so hard that it would surely be frozen shut forever – the flames would overwhelm him.

But the speck called to him. It promised relief.

Strength. More than he'd ever known. Enough to survive. Enough to protect Rikeva, enough to get home. Never reached for the dark, clenching both hands around whatever it was.

Pain vanished.

Fire no longer seared his skin, questing for his bones.

Instead, the flames were a mere fluttering of butterfly wings against his face and arms, against his torso when he rose from his crouch to stare down the Amouni.

Fear grew in their eyes as their arms faltered.

How small each seemed, though none of the Amouni had shrunk. Nor had he grown... yet in a sense, he had. He lifted an arm to point, and the source of the darkness became clear, at last.

Blue skin covered his hand.

Stakolin.

A flicker of horror was smothered quickly; he had a task to complete and Amouni to shame. "Do you wish to yield before I make you?"

His opponents kept up the fire, but the man and woman were beginning to falter, exchanging glances behind Udali.

Udali did not seem to notice; he was speaking to himself, or chewing the inside of his lip as sapphire flame surged forth, merely bouncing from Never's skin.

Perverse joy was gone now. Only doubt remained in the

Amouni's eyes.

"No!" Udali shouted.

Crimson-flame from the others flickered out, and both slumped to the stones. Never approached Udali, movements steady. There was no rush. The man would either fold or be struck down.

Something the fop might even survive, if he was lucky.

Never stopped before Udali, whose hands were still raised, fire still bursting forth, still useless. "Last chance."

And finally, Udali's head fell against his chest as he dropped his arms, fire winking out. "Fine. Fine. You win," he said between hard breaths.

"Say it."

Udali lifted his head, more outrage cutting through the exhaustion as he stood, struggling to keep his feet. "What?"

"Say you yield."

The man's eyes burned with a fresh wave of hate. "I yield."

"Good. Now scurry along." Never gestured to the others. "Don't forget your little friends."

In the silence the followed his victory, Never watched Udali help the others to their feet, shuffling off in a group of stumbles and gasps. Then he strode to Rikeva, whose expression carried traces of doubt. "Never, what was that? Your skin has changed."

"I'll explain soon, but I know what it is. I can control it," he said, despite not knowing one way or another. It *seemed* to be true. Even as he spoke, his skin returned to its usual shade.

If nothing else, it seemed he'd not been deformed.

He glanced around the square. Both soldiers and

Amouni alike now regarded him with new emotions – fear mostly, perhaps grudging respect from some. But he was most interested in one figure in particular; the Rahnzir *had* observed the duel, since Never caught a glimpse of the man slipping behind one of the buildings.

Did the Amouni learn what he wanted to know?

Whether Rahnzir Sarion had arranged the confrontation or whether Udali had simply been unable to help himself, the result was hopefully the same; they all knew exactly who was stronger.

A long time ago, as it seemed, he'd been able to defeat a single stakolin alone.

That did not hold true for other Amouni now. At least, not when the mix of his Amouni and stakolin blood was considered. He'd held out against three Amouni at once, an impressive feat, though he had no desire to discover the upper limit of what he could withstand.

But if he *was* being manipulated, the games were wearing quite thin indeed.

"It seems to have worked," Rikeva said.

"Good." He folded his arms as he regarded those gathered. Most pleasingly, Udali was now being supported by his other fellows. His two lackeys rested upon the stone themselves, attended to by the Amouni.

"I trust this is everyone?"

Rahnzir Sarion approached the *forasa* gate at a stride, his expression stern. In addition to his usual circlet and bracers, he now also wore a golden belt and the protective collar.

The captain met the Amouni with a bow. "Save for those at the Infirmary, Rahnzir."

He nodded. "What of you, Ascended Udali? You and

your force do not seem ready for departure."

The Amouni straightened. "We are, Rahnzir."

"That had better be the truth," he said, voice unforgiving.

"It is, Rahnzir."

"Scarves and collars ready; we'll be landing at the chasm. And for those of you who are new to Hasollea – not only Guardian Never and Rikeva of Marlosi, but any who flew from surrounding posts – I expect you to follow the example of those more experienced with the northern wilds." He paused. "The scouts report calm, but you should expect to be attacked at any time, understood?"

Nods and murmurs of assent answered the man.

# Chapter 21.

Resin in his scarf tinted the gargantuan chasm orange, its depths deepening to a murky red then brown, and eventually black.

Whatever fell from the sky in the past had utterly shattered the land.

Not even the skeletons of trees remained at the edges of the chasm. The edges themselves were difficult to see. While the forest at Never's back was lush, rising to tower over the *forasa* gate, at the far side of the chasm the forest was a mere line of green. It climbed into surrounding mountains, but even they somehow seemed small in comparison to the hole in the very earth.

All barren, where it sloped down toward the crater's edge.

Nearby, the Rahnzir was sending scouts and arranging his soldiers to protect those still passing through the gate. Not a single sapling or scrap of plant-life upon the ground there either. The earth itself was a mixture of black dust and stone, melted and twisted.

"If something is at the bottom, how are the rebels able

to reach it without wings?" Rikeva asked softly. "Is there some endless ladder?"

Never nodded. "Or tunnels."

Rahnzir Sarion lifted his voice from nearby. "You have tasks. For glory of the empire."

Most of the soldiers and Amouni spread out into the forest, moving to ring the chasm, Amouni on their wings, and the royal soldiers in disciplined lines, their bows already drawn.

It left only the Rahnzir and one other; the petulant-faced Udali.

"And us?" Never asked.

"They seek the rebels to buy us time while we discover – and destroy – whatever and whoever is down there."

Never frowned. "And what are we going to destroy? We need at least some idea, don't you think?"

"Of course, Guardian," the man replied with a smile, and a glance to Udali. The Ascended Amouni did not respond, beyond perhaps a slight tightening of his jaw.

Why use the title? It seemed insincere. Especially considering whatever true reason the Rahnzir wanted Never recognised for. "Is my title necessary?"

"For our return, I believe so."

Never shrugged. "Then what of the Shade that is here in the wilds? Is that connected to whatever is below?"

"Their purpose is unknown but they were likely assisting the rebels. However, now they are something far darker."

"Did the survivors share anything useful about that?" Rikeva asked. "Can you at least estimate, based on whatever happened here in the past, recent and distant?"

He glanced to the waiting darkness and motioned for

everyone to follow. "We have time for a brief explanation, I suppose. We still do not know what fell from the sky. But in the years after, new plants grew in the forest; aggressive, deadly plants. The Colony and Amouni fought back, burning what we could." He gestured. "We created this barrier, where nothing will grow, in order to assist locating and destroying Seeds whenever they are heaved up from the depths."

"What of the Seeds themselves?" Never asked.

"Whether inhaled by people or animals, all tend to wither quite quickly. If the husks of the dead are disturbed, more Seeds are scattered to seek fresh victims. They are easy to recognise, of course, being a spotted mix of black and orange. You are each protected, but it is possible to become overwhelmed, even if too many attach themselves to your clothing."

"And what did it do to the Shade?"

"While the Seeds are light and slow-moving, the Shade is not. It killed or deeply wounded the last search party; a score in total, and it could not be stopped. It is as though it can meld with any surface it touches."

"And now we four are descending?"

"Yes."

"Into a pit of endless shadow."

He nodded. "And you will guide us – the Shade will be nothing against your Phoenix Fire."

"And the source of the Seeds?"

"The true enemy. But between us all, I suspect it, too, will fall." He looked to Rikeva. "Especially considering the rather unique powers possessed by your companion."

Rikeva frowned. "I doubt you want me to help whatever is down there to grow."

"No. I refer to the other side of your gift, your Weaving, as I believe you call it."

"What?"

"All things have an opposing side. You may end up being instrumental." The man stopped at the chasm's edge and unfurled his wings, gold gleaming under the morning sun. "Stay close for light," he said as he leapt down.

Udali followed without a word, and Never smiled at Rikeva. "Isn't it fun to learn new things about yourself?"

"I don't know about that." She shook her head. "We'd better catch up."

# Chapter 22.

Never held Rikeva in his arms as they descended, drawing ever-closer to the pair of glowing lights below. That glow ought to have been blue but was far closer to brown thanks to the masks.

Darkness pressed in around him and when he glanced up, the chasm's opening remained enormous but its light did not penetrate far at all. His own glow was enough, just crimson-fire for now, so that Rikeva wouldn't be hurt. For while he could control the crimson's balance of heat and light easily enough, Holy Fire was more volatile.

By the time they caught up to the others, Seeds were rising.

Not a cloud, but enough that he was able to make out detail on more than a few. Each the size of a thumbnail, they were dark but still featured light, swirling patterns. Again, their true colour was difficult to discern due to his mask, but when one of the Seeds struck his leg and remained there like a grass seed, he was pleased for the protection.

"How deep is this chasm?" Never called to the Rahnzir as

he drifted closer.

"While we estimate that the bottom will have its own light source, we cannot know what it will take to reach that point."

Yet no sooner had the man's voice finished echoing when something appeared below, looming at the light's edge. A rock formation? It had grown up from the deep, ending in a domed point. The nearer they drew, the clearer its texture – a scaled surface, possibly green.

More columns of varying shapes and sizes rose as they continued downward, and all too soon, the surfaces were covered in the Seeds, attached by thin, glowing threads. Some columns were large enough to meet at their base, and whenever that happened, the path of descent was blocked. More, pools of dark sludge had built up and whatever lurked beneath tended to move *away* from the fire's glow, their shapes unclear.

As Never detoured yet another blockage, keeping the Amouni reasonably close, he caught sight of something flitting between columns ahead. Yet when they reached the space it had inhabited, there was only a cluster of Seeds. The cluster stretched from a column, threads to breaking point, and accidently formed something of a human shape.

Unless he was wrong.

"Did you see that?" he asked Rikeva.

"No." She'd been examining Seeds upon her sleeves with a frown as more and more were becoming lodged to their clothing, along with the outside of their scarves.

"Maybe nothing then."

He angled his wings to follow the Amouni around a set of the strange, probably living-towers, and entered an open space at last. Other columns were suggestions at the edge of the light, but a clearer path downward seemed probable – at least for a time.

Yet the darkness was also growing stronger, as if to smother their flames.

"Guardian Never. More light."

Never flared his crimson-fire but it made little to no difference. He needed to try the Phoenix flame, but was there a safe way to do so? Perhaps... Ecanseja seemed to know exactly how. A temporary measure only, but so long as Never was willing to sacrifice a dagger...

"Can you reach one of my knives?" he asked Rikeva.

She found one at his hip. "What for?"

"I'm going to make more light – can you hold on to me, for a moment?"

Moving carefully, she wrapped both legs around his waist, her arms sliding around his neck so that they were face-to-face. "Does this work?"

He grinned.

"Idiot. And I can't hold on like this forever."

"It won't take long, if it works. Or if it fails, for that matter." He called the Holy Fire, colours so bright that they seemed white, even through the resin. He let the flame engulf the blade. It melted enough to spread into threads, allowing him to fashion a net of steel, though a net shaped more like a dandelion clock.

But the adjustment to Ecanseja's method for a stationary light seemed as though it would work. He detached the globe of Phoenix fire next, leaving it to cling to the steel – not so different from when attacking, only far, far gentler.

Finally, Never tossed the reforged dagger out.

It hung in the air for but a moment, lighting their surrounds enough to see more columns. And then the lamp fell, gaining speed and vanishing too swiftly to be of any real use.

"Is that the best you can manage?" Udali called back.

Never glared down at the man. "Shut up." Then, to Rikeva, he asked a question that would hopefully solve the problem. "Can you pluck a feather, for me?"

She reached behind him, and her fingers took a firm grip on one of the quills. "Ready?"

"I am."

She yanked it free.

He winced but accepted the feather with a nod. This time, he created another make-shift lamp of bright, glowing steel in the shape of a flower, but built it around the feather. Would it work? Only one way to be sure. He threw his second lamp out and, blessedly, it fell at a much gentler pace.

Easily enough to match, not that Never expected any thanks.

Nor did he receive it, as the Amouni simply continued down, their own fires adding to the fight against the shadow.

Udali flinched.

His light blinked out. Never frowned down at the man, and then his eyes widened. Something had burst through the Amouni's back, having speared up from below...

"Scatter!" roared the Rahnzir.

# Chapter 23.

Never banked sharply, keeping a tight grip on Rikeva as Udali's body plummeted to vanish into shadow.

In the silence, Never kept weaving, muscles tense as he hovered just beyond the edge of the lamplight – or so he hoped.

At the same time, he'd doused his fire. Was that even the safe thing to do?

The Rahnzir was no-where to be seen, and as Never urged Rikeva to hold on, a faint splat rose from below. Either Udali had struck another column or the bottom was closer than it seemed.

"Can you sense whatever that was?" Rikeva whispered.

"No. You?"

"I don't think so."

"We need to see what's down there," he said. "As soon as we land, I'll call the Holy Fire again, bright as I can. Stay close, but once we know what we're facing, be ready to run. Or attack, I suppose."

She nodded, then rested her chin upon his shoulder. "Let

me watch your back."

Down they floated.

Tension continued to tighten every muscle, especially his wings. And they'd been locked in place for long enough without the threat of being skewered from the darkness. His arms too, were tiring. Though with Rikeva clinging to him now, they'd been given something of a rest.

Before too long, the lantern he'd made came to settle upon the chasm's bottom.

Or an enormous plateau.

The light didn't reveal their attacker but it was enough to see Udali's broken wings, along with a mess of dark blood splattered beneath the man's body.

The ground was mostly stone with only the occasional Seed, although some parts featured more black patches that did not seem to be blood, patches that continued beyond the light's limit. There, the base of something large, still hidden in shadow, waited without sound or movement.

Never touched down.

Rikeva found her feet but didn't let go. Instead, she leant in to kiss him – a brief moment only – then released him. "Ready when you are."

He exhaled. "Here we go."

Twin-coloured flame burst across his body. He let it sear the air around him – enough to illuminate their surroundings comfortably.

Hissing echoed from above.

Thin, human-like creatures clamoured across a tower-like column. Far too sprightly to be Leschnilef, their heads were a little bulbous, faces difficult to discern. Most disappeared into openings of varying sizes, and which offered an answering glow from deep within.

No signs of whatever had killed Udali.

"Are they actually human?" Rikeva asked, staff in hand.

"We'll probably have to find out." He glanced around. Still no sign of the attacker, nor the Rahnzir for that matter. And by now, all the creatures had returned to the tower, leaving behind only a few floating Seeds.

The column bore no steps, but the lowest entry point was not impossible to reach, which also had the added benefit of being more than large enough to walk within. Stooped, probably, but better than a blank wall.

Never kept his Phoenix-fire ablaze, but eased off, creating deeper shadows. Counting the lamp light and his own hands, it would still be enough to search for whatever threat lay inside – another vagary from the Amouni that would have to be dealt with. "We don't know if Sarion survived and I can't wait to fly out of this pit, so let's not hesitate any longer."

"I agree," Rikeva said.

Together, they climbed into the column. The surface was firmer than fish scales beneath his grip, more like bark, in some ways. A strong scent penetrated his scarf, like nothing he could describe, but hopefully it was no poison.

He led Rikeva deeper through the first tunnel, ignoring side-passages as he headed for the answering glow. If the creatures had dug their way inside, it had been uneven work – supposing they had tools.

There was always a chance they tunnelled their way *out*.

Scratching sounds drifted down from above, but he ignored them, heading for the centre. There, a soft glow was revealed as reflected light struck a dome of liquid. It pulsed steadily, dominating a huge chamber that, like the tunnels, appeared to have been hewn free by claws.

Three figures swam within the clear dome, mostly silhouettes.

And clearly, no rebel was responsible for what he was witnessing. They may have benefitted from it somehow, but they could not be behind it. Not at all human, the creatures were far too slender. They were almost like blades of grass, with vague limbs and torsos linked by the same threads he'd seen elsewhere. The threads gleamed, connecting not only limbs to bodies, but figures to each other *and* connecting all three to the dome's base.

"Never, look." Rikeva was pointing up.

Seeds covered the inner walls of the column.

They reached the limit of his light, and considering how densely the Seeds clung to the surface, probably far beyond. And they were several layers deep, surely.

Never flared the flames a little higher, confirming that the Seeds continued on.

Poised to burst forth.

Up and out of the chasm, to spread and smother the forest and people above. And if what had grown across the decades to become what lay before him was any indication, the dome was enough to destroy a city, as promised.

Maybe more.

# Chapter 24.

"How do we destroy this?" Rikeva asked. "Will fire be enough? Can we do it without becoming poisoned?"

Never strode closer but did not touch the clear dome. "I hope so." He glanced over his shoulder and found no crowd of thin creatures poised to attack. In fact, he could no longer hear their movements above. A good sign, or a terrible omen?

"What do you need me to do?" Rikeva asked.

"Guard the tunnel, just in case. And if I collapse, pull me out."

"Of course." She stepped back.

Never exhaled. This time, it would be a memory of Snow that he called on, rather than Ecanseja. Back in the Temple of Jyan, Snow had obliterated the ceiling, and this column would only serve to funnel flames higher and farther.

He drew in all the fire he could – a mix of crimson and the Holy Fire – and fed the boiling blaze that built up with traces of awakened stakolin blood. Never let his skin darken to blue as he did, then flung his arms into the air.

An eruption.

It roared up the column. Glimpses of Seeds vanished in a searing inferno, some drifting down as mere specks of ash. More than enough to drive him on; it was working. He kept the flame surging forth longer, longer, longer, until even with the help of the stakolin taint, he began to flag.

Using the Phoenix-flame came at a higher cost, but he wasn't finished.

Never swung his twin flames at the dome.

Steam burst free.

He moved closer, concentrating heat as the dome shrank, smaller and smaller, steam still surging up and out. The figures within thrashed wildly, but he did not let up. Not until all three had collapsed, and then, not until they – and the dome – were mere smudges of soot resting in the centre of the column.

He cut the fire, leaving only enough crimson curled around one fist in order to see.

Never blinked as the room spun, but he kept his feet.

Then Rikeva had an arm around him. "It worked."

"Good, good."

She led him back into the tunnel. He stumbled several times but soon enough, they were outside, back to where the lamp still shone. "Just a moment." He lowered himself to the cold stone. "I just need to rest a little."

She knelt at his side, and once again she had her staff ready.

But no-one attacked, nor even appeared.

Not until Never caught his breath – enough to look around, at least. From the upper reaches of the dark column, a line of the spindly creatures approached, still clinging to the surface as they moved… dozens, all in all.

Rikeva stood. "I don't know how long I can hold them off."

But the creatures were not hissing, moving only slowly. No change when they reached the ground either. Instead, they formed single file then moved to arrange themselves in a circle several rows deep around the lamp.

One at a time, each went to their knees and lay back next, facing the distant, invisible sky. If that was the correct term since their faces were not faces at all, but bulbous shapes.

He reached for Rikeva's hand, and she helped him upright. "What is this?"

"It was almost a procession," she replied.

The creatures had grown motionless, not even a twitch from a single one.

"We need to know if they're a threat," Rikeva said.

He nodded, and with Rikeva still supporting his steps, they approached the creatures, the nearest of which bore blackened marks on its pear-shaped head. The burnt figure, like the others, remained utterly still.

Never gasped when they stopped before it.

Several layers of… leaves had unfurled from around the head, half-seared away. It revealed part of a face; a human's cheek and mouth, with just a glimpse of a single, wide and staring eye.

Rikeva drew him down as she knelt. "Never… I don't know why, but I think they want *me* to save them."

"Then… is that even possible?"

"It might be." She pushed up one sleeve and unwound a ribbon… then stopped with a deep frown. "Sarion said there was an opposite, right?"

"He did. But does he know your gift better than you?"

"Enough to open my eyes to a possibility, I guess," she replied with a rueful smile. Then she extended both hands over the singed figure, and closed her eyes.

At first, nothing changed, leaving Never with the sound of his own breathing only.

But then, the leaves began to unfurl.

Movement around the head revealed a young Arathona man, and then the leaves split downward to reveal his naked chest. Welts remained whenever a leaf fell away, blackening as it curled.

"It's working, Rika," he said with his own smile.

She kept going until the man was free, then moved to the second prisoner. And already she was moving faster – just like when she'd worked on the arch-blossoms to cure Oleksan's decay.

The first fellow blinked where he lay, remaining unmoving otherwise. Yet it seemed his lips curved in a faint smile.

Rikeva was already onto the next victim, this time an Amouni woman.

"I don't think that's necessary." Rahnzir Sarion stumbled into the light, his face and arms covered in bloody bruises. Had he fought off whatever killed Udali?

Despite seeming to stand on his last legs, the Rahnzir raised both hands.

Never dove for Rikeva.

Blue fire roared.

He wrapped her in his arms and rolled free from the flames with a curse.

Fury drove him back to his feet, Rikeva at his side just

as swiftly. Only piles of ash remained nearby, where the chasm's victims had once lain in the hope of being saved.

"Animal!" Rikeva cried.

Never caught her arm as she charged, and the look in her eye nearly drove him back a step. "Together," he told her, hoping she would understand.

And she did; nodding, her jaw clenched.

"Your sentiment is a sign of your weakness, and typical of your kind." Sarion sneered from where he stood before wrapping one arm around his side. "They would spread more Seeds or create more death and undo all that we achieved here."

There was no point responding.

Never called the Holy Fire, and Rikeva hefted her staff – her muscles having already grown. "Flank him." Never sent a stream of Holy Fire – twisting blue and green – at the Amouni.

Sarion leapt aside, yet it was more of a stumble due to whatever injury he'd suffered.

Flames tore half the man's leg from his body.

Before the Amouni could even scream, Rikeva crashed her staff into his head. Bone shattered, blood splattering across stone.

The Rahnzir's lifeless body slumped to the ground.

# Chapter 25.

Never lay upon stony earth, Rikeva beside him, the light of day welcome upon his face. The slight breeze was another sweet blessing – he'd removed the scarf and seared it of the Seeds but hadn't been willing to close his eyes and fully relax just yet, not until he was certain no Seeds would drift too near.

Or that no over-zealous Amouni would appear, demanding to know where the Rahnzir was.

"Are you in too much pain?" Rikeva asked.

His wings burned where he lay, his shoulders and torso too – his arms, everything. All of it was aflame, but he could rest now.

For a few moments, anyway.

Then, he had to haul himself upright and reach the dark arch, which was not so far yet seemed to rest an unfathomable distance away.

"Yes. But it's worth it to be out of that hole."

A shadow blocked the sun, and a familiar voice spoke. "Please."

He rose; Guardian Min stood before them, her body once again trembling. Pink pollen hung around her figure and petals drifted from her hands and forearms now, but she had not succumbed to the *semir-ko*.

The woman didn't seem poised to strike.

"Never, let me."

Rikeva climbed to her feet, moving with purpose. He nodded as she reached out to take the Guardian's face into her hands, speaking softly. "I will try."

The woman blinked, pink tears running down her cheeks.

Rikeva closed her eyes, her palms still cradling the Guardian. And just like in the depths of the chasm, something was changing.

The woman's eyes were reverting to their original blue.

Petals drifted from her hands and forearms, twisting and curling into tiny buds of brown and black as they hit the earth. It revealed the Guardian's natural skin and as if in response, the tattoos grew darker on her upper arms.

Rikeva shifted her hands to take the Guardian's own, and still more pink drained away. Her knees buckled at one point, but Never caught her. "Rika?"

"It's fine, I can save her," she said as she leant against his chest, but did not let go of the Guardian, her gift working still.

Never checked on Guardian Min and the woman was smiling now, the only traces of the *semir-ko* left being thin rings of pink beneath her eyes. "You already did, Rikeva."

Rikeva sighed and her weight grew heavier as she fell into an exhausted sleep, or so he hoped. Thankfully, she was definitely breathing. He ran his fingers across her cheek.

"Let me help you both now," the Guardian said.

More shadows passed over them. Never looked up with a frown, several Amouni were swooping down to land. Half a dozen in all, and none of them wearing welcoming expressions. At least one was a familiar face, the pale woman from Udali's ill-fated duel. "Rahnzir Sarion is dead. Ascended Udali too. Guardians or no, we will have answers from you."

If they knew as much already, it didn't seem that lying would make any difference. Not now, and not to the Conclave – their likely destination.

"The source of the Seeds killed Udali before we landed," he replied. "The creature that controlled the Seeds had taken prisoners. We began to restore the victims, at which point Sarion appeared and slaughtered them. We executed him after that."

Silence met his words.

Finally, the pale woman spoke. "Prisoners?"

"I do not know if they were all rebels, but both Arathona and Amouni," he replied. "We also destroyed the source of the Seeds, along with an amount easily enough to overwhelm Hasollea many times over. Should any of you be brave enough to descend the chasm, this can all be confirmed simply enough."

One of the Amouni lowered his voice. "Fijeso, I think we can all feel that the threat has nearly vanished."

She frowned. "Send someone down there. Enough to carry Ascended Udali and Rahnzir Sarion home, at least. Investigate every detail."

"Take plenty of light," Never added.

Fijeso directed her frown to Guardian Min. "Guardian, you remain infected and will be isolated until such a time as you may fully recover."

"Of course," she replied. "However, Guardian Never – if that is to be his standing when all evidence has been assessed – will need to be taken to Conclave Esuta immediately."

"In light of –"

"That is the wish of the Conclave," Guardian Min interrupted.

Fijeso gave a short nod. "As you will it, Guardian."

## Chapter 26.

Never had been afforded little chance to speak to Rikeva or Guardian Min. A dozen Amouni that included Fijeso had kept them moving too swiftly, passing through a rapid succession of *forasa* until finally coming to a halt in yet another room of white.

Unlike so many others, here the bright-blue quartz was joined by thinner streaks of green. It still could have been the Eastern Palace, or it could have been somewhere else entirely, there was no way to know.

His questions went largely unanswered, and Guardian Min was immediately taken elsewhere. Her final words were of encouragement, however. "Conclave Esuta is a powerful voice. She will be pleased, even if Rahnzir Sarion did not survive."

And then they were alone, sealed in a room that no longer bore even the hint of usual doors able to slide open via touch.

Rikeva had recovered enough to pace, and Never nearly joined her. Instead, he leant against the wall, folded his arms and tapped his fingers against a bicep.

"Are you sure we've done enough to satisfy them?" she asked.

"No."

"Part of me thinks we have – if they weren't Amouni."

"They *should* be in our debt, even taking into account killing Sarion."

She nodded. "But we can't trust them. And now Min has been isolated."

A definite concern.

"What about your plan to burn our way to freedom should we need?" she asked, after coming to a halt.

He met her gaze. "I don't know how much Holy Fire I could use, not so soon after the chasm. If we needed –"

The door slid open.

Two Amouni entered, their faces quite stern but offering no real clues as to their standing. They flanked the doorway, allowing a figure draped in white robes and golden lace to glide within.

Conclave Esuta at last? Or another member of the mysterious ruling class?

The figure beckoned Never closer, and as before, rested a cloth-covered hand upon his shoulder. *Accept my thanks for all that you have achieved – you have saved a great many Amouni lives with your actions.*

It was her. And no mention of Sarion yet; perhaps it shouldn't have been a surprise considering the general disregard Amouni had for those deemed 'lesser'. Never nodded. "I trust that means you are able to speak to the rest of the Conclave on our behalf?"

*Assuredly. Understand that you will be questioned before the*

*Seat of Facets separately.*

Never relayed her words to Rikeva, who moved to his side. "Why?"

*Merely tradition.*

Again, he shared what he was told.

*However, you must be warned. Those to follow cannot be trusted – they mean to hold your companion to ransom. Do not let this come to pass.*

"Who?" Never asked.

*Factions within the Conclave that do not approve of what we are trying to achieve.*

She lifted her hand then began to drift back toward the door. She ignored his demand for more answers. Her words were plausible enough… weren't they? The woman was already in the hall, her Guards joining her, the door sliding shut.

Rikeva gripped his arm. "Never, what did she say?"

"That whoever comes through that door next will hold you as ransom."

The panel slid open once more.

Five Amouni, all bearing similar circlets and lattice-work on their bracers. All Rahnzir, clearly. Four sets of clear blue eyes, one green, and little else to tell them apart save for the fact that two may have been women. Never was uncertain, based on their gleaming hair and fine features.

Far more concerning was their purpose.

"Guardian Never and Rikeva of Marlosi, you are summoned." It was one of the men who spoke, his voice sharp. "The Conclave will interrogate you separately."

"Wait," Never said. "We do not agree to that."

"Your assent is not relevant." One of the others stepped

toward Rikeva, and Never moved to intercept – only to hit the floor as if hurled down by some unseen force.

A Rahnzir face loomed over him with a frown. "Control yourself."

Rikeva shouted, writhing against invisible bonds – Esuta hadn't been lying! Holy Fire burst from his body, driving them back. But one by one, the Rahnzir raised their hands to cover their hearts.

His flame vanished.

A crushing pressure replaced it and he struggled to breathe. One of the Rahnzir collapsed but was quickly supported by their fellows. The remaining Amouni had already ringed Rikeva in a cage of blue fire. Someone started to drag him from the room – his limbs still rigid, his gaze restricted now. Not even able to turn his head, he could no longer see Rikeva, couldn't respond when she called his name, since even his face was frozen.

The corridors outside were more of the endless, smooth white. Some muttered curses as they dragged him along, others complaining about the Conclave. Or about certain members only? He couldn't tell, and the pressure on his body had hardly eased, the force enough that his fingers and toes were beginning to bend.

They slid him into another room, with only two Rahnzir joining him.

One removed a coil of lilac rope and began to bind him with a sneer. "Nothing more than a filthy Stray."

Still, he could not respond.

But Never's limbs *were* loosening – they had to, in order for the man to tie his arms behind his back, and for one of the women to arrange his feet and then affix silver shackles.

Finally, the Amouni hauled him to his feet.

Standing was difficult, but he managed with the support of a captor.

The Rahnzir who'd announced the interrogation appeared, holding a gag. He tied it around Never's head with a frown, then motioned for the others to follow him outside. This time, the door did not slide closed, and Never could easily hear them.

"Once the Conclave is ready, send for Guards. I'll join them."

"How long?"

"Soon. Just ensure that he doesn't bleed out."

"Of course."

Never wanted to frown – deeply. Bleed out? From what? The lilac blocked him from calling his flame, as it had back in the Temple Trivium, but how would it cause bleeding? After all, he wasn't feeling worse, and he could already stand for himself.

No sooner had he finished his thought, when something warm pooled in his hands.

Blood?

One of the Rahnzir returned, immediately breaking into a frown. He withdrew a thin knife and stopped before Never. "I am going to monitor your bleeding – from the state of your clothes, you have far more wounds than expected."

Still Never could not answer.

The Amouni cut away his tunic, movements careful – likely so as not to touch any blood – and revealed more wounds. Old scars had reopened, blood seeping forth with a pain he couldn't yet feel. How? What had been done to him when the Rahnzir collapsed before?

"Are you acting confused, or do you really hail from a time yet to come?"

Never frowned.

"You should know what is happening – this is how all Strays are captured."

"What?" Never could finally speak.

Now the Amouni shrugged. "Only, it doesn't usually take five of us."

The first Rahnzir appeared in the doorway, flanked by two Guards. "Bring him."

# Chapter 27.

"The mongrel that refers to himself as 'Never' will approach the Seat of Facets."

Never glared up toward the disembodied voice where it spoke from somewhere within the shadowy hall – a fine contrast, considering all of the white elsewhere. Chains clinked as he shuffled forward. Blood trickled across his skin from barely-healed wounds that covered his half-naked body.

Wounds that refused to heal.

Old wounds, reopened.

The glare was all he could manage in the way of defiance, considering the gag of lilac-soaked cloth that stung his tongue and seared his airways. Not to mention the lilac ropes that bound him.

The Conclave sat arranged in such a way that their faces and robed-torsos remained in shadow, with only hands resting upon their knees visible – and even those very hands seemed covered by the robes.

The voice, the owner of which remained hidden,

continued to speak for the Conclave.

"Offer both Apologies and Regret. Do so, and you may be permitted to select the form of your execution."

Not an interrogation at all.

Footsteps approached from behind and someone removed the gag.

"I did not aid you all in order to apologise," he said. "Will the Conclave speak?"

"Only if they choose."

Never kept his voice even. "Conclave Esuta, we have saved the Spring Colony and achieved all you asked – I await your words."

Light glowed around the fourth chair, leaving the other eleven in their customary half-darkness.

*Fellow Conclave members. Let it be known that I do not recognise this man.*

For a moment, her words did not register.

*Yet I am aware of various transgressions committed under my name. Most grievous of which, being the murder of Rahnzir Sarion.*

Never clenched his hands into fists; exactly the betrayal he should have expected! Was Sarion involved from the beginning? The Supreme? The young man had been instrumental in bringing Esuta to them. And Guardian Min, what of her… Had she been duped as well?

No-one could be trusted.

From the dark, a new voice answered Esuta – a man, his tone curt. *Explain yourself, Conclave Esuta.*

*Of course,* she replied. *Rahnzir Sarion sought cooperation of the mongrel in order to save the Spring Colony. While Sarion succeeded, it appears to have cost him his life. Witnesses are available, should you wish to hear from them.*

And Never knew exactly who they would be.

Another chair spoke, also from the dark. *Should we let the mongrel speak?*

*Why?*

Several voices answered at once.

Conclave Esuta's raised voice rang in his mind. *I remind you that I still have the Light.*

Quiet followed.

*I do not believe he should speak. We are all aware that Rahnzir Oripa is still unconscious after being forced to activate the Confinement.*

Esuta's timely 'warning' had obviously been the final part of her ploy – the perfect way to force his hand into what would appear to be an attack on the Rahnzir, at a time when he was feeling most distrustful.

*I also remind you that this is a dangerous man; a man who attacked the Rahnzir mere moments ago, a man whose blood is the most unclean in all recorded history. Furthermore, in the few days since he attacked Temple Trivium, he has already robbed vendors, threatened innkeepers, refused to investigate the sighting of a Shade, assaulted those he was to fight beside, murdered one of those Ascended, murdered a* Rahnzir *and all of it whilst pretending to work under my direction. No. I refuse to have such a mark appear against my good name – he needs no voice.*

Never spat. It really was a meticulously-planned swindle.

Gasps rose, and the gag was quickly replaced.

An answer to Conclave Esuta's litany of transgressions came from a papery voice. *I request the Light.* Darkness covered the betrayer as light switched to the new speaker. Again, it revealed nothing about the specific Conclave member, merely more white cloth and the glimmer of gold. *Can these claims be conclusively substantiated? The mongrel's blood notwithstanding.*

*That very blood may well prove useful.* Another speaker interjected.

*Then we drain him.* Yet another voice Never did not recognise – but he cared not. There was only one speaker he was listening for, and only one question he would ask when he could.

Esuta answered. *Yes, they can be proven.*

The papery voice sighed. *Then we deliberate on draining or outright destruction of his blood, body and bones. Send him to the pit until we have a resolution.*

Hands dragged Never by the shoulders. He wrenched free, blood splattering from his wounds – but once again, an unseen force drove him to the stones.

Never glared up at Conclave Esuta.

And this time, the pressure grew until his vision dimmed…

***

…Never woke to dim light. It barely illuminated the pit of stone he'd been crammed into, his knees almost pressed against his chest. The gag and the lilac ropes were gone, but his body was caked in blood – some of it layers deep.

Little seemed fresh, as best he could tell. A pitifully small mercy.

He craned his neck.

The light came from a lamp that would have been just

out of reach, had he bothered. His mouth screamed for water, but all he had to swallow was blood.

Movement seemed far too much, anyway.

Even his fury was faint beneath the exhaustion. Another thing beyond his grasp. Which didn't mean that he no longer wanted the Amouni dead. Or that he wouldn't have relished tearing Esuta into pieces, but there was just no strength left in his body to summon rage much less fire – be it crimson, holy, or otherwise.

"Rika. I'm sorry."

Each word tore at his throat, as though inhaling the strange, lilac-soaked gag for so long had wounded him there too.

He tried to make a fist but his fingers were weak.

To die now!

To die now, trapped in a distant past, without ever discovering whether his friends had survived or if they had simply vanished thanks to Oleksan's madness – to know he'd failed them... to know he'd failed *all* peoples in *all* lands. And to know he'd failed Rikeva too.

Tears trickled down his cheeks.

The floor gave way.

Never fell with a shout only to strike stone hard enough to cut his cry short. A hunk of rock thudded into his stomach next, other pieces crashing down around him in a cloud of dust.

For a moment, all he could do was appreciate being able to stretch his limbs, his back and neck.

A hushed voice thanked someone, and then the sound of scurrying footfalls followed. They faded swiftly, leaving smaller sounds in their place, boots crossing stone;

crunching upon small pieces as they neared.

"Never. Can you hear me?" A hand rested upon his shoulder. He turned his head, and for the second time in recent days, found Guardian Min looking down at him. This time, her eyes were full of worry.

"Water."

She lifted a vial of clear liquid. He squinted at it; faint traces of yellow crossed the vial like webs, and when she lifted it to his lips, a sweet scent nearly overwhelmed him. "Drink this, quickly. It will be enough for you to fly, if needed."

With no other option, Never drank.

Most sweet was not the scent, but a soothing coolness that slid down his throat. He finished the vial and gasped in relief.

"You should be able to stand. We need to find Rikeva."

Upon hearing her name, he rose... and his limbs were no longer aching with cramps or dull from numbness. More, his strength was already returning.

Whatever the liquid contained, it was powerful – far more potent even than the strongest dose of *batena*.

A dim tunnel built from old stone of uneven construction offered few clues as to exactly where he stood, and certainly not to the question of why Guardian Min was helping him, but he was ready to move; the draught having worked its magic. "Where is she?"

"Follow me. We have a tiny chance of this working." The woman set off at a jog; a soft new light moving with her.

Never dragged his legs into action, finally catching up and finding himself able to keep pace easily enough. "Where is she?"

"Merely a locked room. It's not far, but we might need

a way to move about unseen once we return to the upper floors."

"Well, I'm out of ideas."

She stopped, taking his arm – the first time one of the Amouni had shown no hesitation to come into contact with his blood. "Please. I called in nearly every favour and debt I could in order to get this far."

He frowned back at the Guardian, but the gesture of her touch was more convincing than her words. Maybe she could be trusted, after all, perhaps she was a victim, too. "No-one will buy you having captured two escapees… We need something to draw their attention."

"Nothing is larger than your arrival, not in the city, and not in the previous ten or twenty years, Never."

"Not even the assassination of the Fountain?"

She narrowed her eyes. "Impossible."

"Then something else – you hold all the knowledge of this time."

"Let me think then. We'll keep moving." She set off once more into the dark of the tunnel, the tongue of flame she held lighting the way.

True to her word, it did not take long to reach a flight of stairs. She passed first one and then two doors of steel, both set off from the stair, not stopping until she reached a third door. This time, it was made of the usual white steel or stone.

"Here?" he asked.

She nodded, and moving quietly, led him along a well-lit corridor and to the nearest intersecting passage before slipping into an empty room. It bore only chairs and table beneath a large window.

"Well?" Never asked.

"We are only a few doors from where Rikeva is being kept."

He frowned. Their surrounds hardly seemed like a prison. Even being near the so-called 'pit'. More likely, since the Amouni considered her 'common' and therefore no threat, there was no need to move her to a proper cell. It could well have been a busy part of the palace, and so he drew the curtains to make sure that no passersby in the garden beyond could glance within and notice them.

"So, do you have an idea, yet?"

Min was shaking her head, though her words were more hopeful. "I may."

"Tell me."

"We use the Guides. I can call one and tell them I have seen a Shade. Then, I'll command the Guide to share a warning throughout the palace – all those nearby will have to leave their posts to search. Any Rahnzir will recognise the ruse soon enough. But we should be able to flee the city at least."

"Good enough. How do we find a *forasa*?"

"In fact…" She hesitated. "I believe that I can create one here. Or fashion one, at least."

Impressive. "Is that even possible?"

"Your father managed to do so by grafting disused or faded *forasa* together. Now that I've witnessed it, I believe I can replicate his process."

"You saw that in my blood?"

"Among other things. I am sorry that you lived through so much suffering, Never."

He smiled, though it did not last. "If your plan works, I

won't have to suffer much longer."

She nodded as she took her belt knife and sliced into her palm. Then, she knelt upon the carpet and drew the five-pointed leaf in blood. "This is more an anchor point rather than a true *forasa*."

"Do you need my help?"

"You need to rest longer. The venom is the only thing keeping you going right now."

"Venom?"

"Yes." She moved her hands in a repeated motion, as if drawing strands of something near. "Its effects are temporary. As Amouni, you will not be harmed."

Min kept working, and the longer he watched, the easier it was to see silvery threads being gathered. By the time she stopped, it was a normal, glittering *forasa* – far better work than that which Father had done.

"It won't last long." She called a Guide, this one bearing a lion's head, and issued her instructions.

*Yes, Master.*

As on the streets of Hasollea, the emotionless voice of the Guides – several from what Never could hear – began to issue the false warning. It urged all to search the southern gardens for a Shade, no matter their role or current task.

Footsteps echoed as someone left their post at a run.

Her ploy had worked.

Never slipped into the white corridor, pausing before the door Min indicated. "Will it open for me?"

A mighty crack echoed from within the room, enough to feel a rumble through the floor. Never slapped his hand against the door's panel, flakes of blood flying, and charged inside.

Light poured through a gaping hole in the far wall; white stone and blue quartz alike in a mess upon the floor.

Rikeva was climbing through when she paused, looking over her shoulder. "Never?"

He had to grin. "I see that we're a little late."

She crossed the room at a run and he caught her in his arms. "I had a plan, you know."

"We've got one too," he replied. "A *forasa* in the next room."

"It won't last much longer," Min said from the doorway. "Quickly."

# Chapter 28.

The Kiymako *forasa* Min had chosen was in a somewhat more isolated position than Never had expected, but it was clearly the correct choice. The Guardian travelled with a half-naked man covered in dried blood, and soon enough, all Amouni would be seeking them.

But it was not so isolated that there was *nothing* nearby. Below, visible through the black pines, waited the rooves of a small village, along with several jetties, all empty. Birds chattered above, somewhere out of sight – a bright and welcome sound.

Guardian Min's eyes were alight with her success as she spoke. "I will make another *forasa* and set a false trail." She pointed below, then set to work. "The village has been abandoned for some years since the Kiymako moved their capital from nearby. You will be safe there until I return."

"When?"

"As soon as possible. But if I'm not back by midday tomorrow, then you'll know that I have been imprisoned." She paused, glanced between them both. "If that happens, then I wish you success in your quest to return home and I will always remember you. Above all, Rikeva, I owe you a debt."

And then she was gone before Rikeva could respond.

"I hope she does return," Rikeva said, staring down at the *forasa*, which was already fading.

"Seems like she really was the only one we could trust," Never replied.

"Without her…"

He put a hand on her shoulder. "Let's find some shelter."

Together, they picked a way down overgrown animal trails, accompanied by the welcome scent of the pines, and soon entered the abandoned village.

Splitting up to search, Never found a barren garden before the first home he checked. Inside, empty shelves, broken furniture and a thin layer of dust on all that remained, including a broken canister painted with a detailed vision of the forest.

Neither bedroom contained any useful bedding. He moved on to the next house, this one much smaller, only to find similar debris. Next was a home that had been abandoned before construction was complete. He sighed, in part due to his failure to find anything useful, in part due to the growing weariness in his legs.

Outside, he met Rikeva in the small square, where a covered well stood. "The water seems safe," she said.

"I can't say I had any success with the homes I checked."

She gestured over her shoulder. "The one with the stable has a basement we can use. Looters must have missed it; it was well-hidden."

"Wonderful. Let me just take a dip in the ocean, and then

I think I need to lie down a moment. Whatever Min gave me is wearing off."

"What about your wounds?"

"Hopefully closed."

"I'll do some foraging in the woods and start on a meal," she said, heading toward the trees.

Never moved to the nearest jetty where the ocean lapped against the shore. The water stretched toward the afternoon sun. It could have been named the Sea of Stars, as one day it would be, but there was no-one to ask. He removed his shoes, then stepped into the shallows, submerging himself with a pre-emptive grimace… only to find that most of his wounds had closed.

Most.

The saltwater still stung enough in places, but he washed his hair as best he could, rubbing the dried blood from his torso and his pants too, before hauling himself out of the water. Then he made his way across uneven boards to the end of the jetty, letting a soft breeze dry him, swaying slightly on his feet.

And it wasn't until his skin was dry, and he'd taken a few steps toward the home Rikeva had pointed out, that he realised he'd been standing very much out in the open. Had anyone been watching the village, they would be discovered.

Amouni or no, anyone – if they wanted – could surprise him while he slept.

And sleep was what he was craving.

Even Rikeva's promise of food wasn't enough to stop him shambling through the large house and climbing down a hatch to the basement. She'd described it as being hidden, but he couldn't tell exactly what she'd done to uncover it; his vision wasn't too clear.

But he managed to find a bed with blankets that seemed to have survived quite well – and they were certainly cool and soft when he collapsed against them with a sigh.

***

Never woke to warm firelight and mostly darkness.

It was not a blazing fire, being just enough to heat a pot. The scent of vegetables with rosemary drifted his way, easily sufficient to have him sit up. His stomach rumbled as he moved.

Rikeva turned from where she sat beyond the flame, her face softened by the light. She must have been just as tired as he. More, by now. "How are you feeling?" she asked.

"Good. Enough to fly, enough to call fire if we need it. I can watch now, if you want to sleep."

"Once you've eaten, I think I'll take you up on that offer."

"No sign of trouble? Or Min?"

"Not yet."

Impossible to say what had happened. Min *had* asked them to wait until midday tomorrow, so there was certainly still a chance she'd not been captured. Or worse.

Never accepted the bowl Rikeva handed him and started on the meal as she took the bed. The vegetables were a little overcooked, suggesting that he'd slept for some time, but the warmth that spread throughout his body was a more than satisfactory compensation.

In the quiet that followed after he'd finished, he stared into the flames. And it took longer than it ought to have done, but he finally realised that they were alone. Alone, and probably as safe as they would be until they got home.

Never turned to the bed.

"Rikeva?"

"I'm awake. Is something wrong?"

He knelt at her side, and leant in, until his face was close to hers. "How about a game of tira-tra?"

She smiled and drew his face closer; their lips met.

Never deepened their kiss.

Rika pulled him near, and he trailed his lips along her cheek and down her neck, the scent of her filling his mind. He ran a hand across her body, slipping under her tunic… and found more ribbons.

She grinned. "No need to rush, but why don't you help me with them?"

"Of course."

He straightened as she extended a leg. The ribbons started at her ankle and led up toward her thigh.

He began to unwind the first strip of fabric with a smile.

# Chapter 29.

Morning came and passed without Min's return. While waiting, they ate a sparse breakfast and filled the time by completing small tasks in the basement, using what light filtered down from above.

"If we have to leave without Min, do you know where we are in relation to the Phoenix?" Rikeva asked. She was adjusting the steel tip of her staff, sitting cross-legged upon the floor by the bed.

For a moment, Never let himself imagine a life where it was possible to simply lift her back to the bed, a life where if he left a room, he could do so for no other purpose than to find something beautiful for her...

Instead of the relentless uncertainty that actually had to be faced.

They were yet to discuss last night, but was there any need to rush? It was enough to wake happy, enough to wake feeling closer to her. To use the respite, no matter how short it might be, on hope and idle thoughts of a bright future.

Returning home suddenly meant so much more.

It could be the beginning of a new life; a different life, if he wanted it. If Rikeva wanted it too – and it seemed she did. He'd find a way to make it happen, even if it meant burning his way through every Amouni that dared stand before them.

"I do. The Cesanha Mountains were on the eastern coast, that's where the egg lies. Or the Great Phoenix herself, I hope. I'm not sure what we'll find."

"You mean, she could be… dormant?"

"Possibly. I hadn't thought to ask anyone. I suppose Guardian Min will know."

"Then let's wait a little longer."

"Right. I'll check outside, in case she's looking for us." Never tied off the final stitch in the makeshift tunic he'd made from half the blanket, a fairly rudimentary thing of pale blue. He slipped it over his head as he stood. "How does it look?"

She laughed. "Adequate."

"I'm no tailor, as you know."

"Well, you don't have to be, so don't feel too bad," she said. "I'll gather anything useful while you search."

He nodded, and climbed up to the ground floor, leaving the hatch open before slipping into the deserted streets… and there, at the far end of the village, a figure was actually leaving, striding toward an outlying home.

Guardian Min!

Never called her name and she turned, approaching at a jog. "You were safe here?"

"We were. Seems like your diversion was successful."

She nodded. "So far. I was able to leave more than

one trail. It ought to work, but the Conclave will spare no expense seeking you. They may be waiting at the Great Phoenix."

"I'll be ready for that, thanks to that venom."

"As I'd hoped," she replied with a smile. "Guardians sometimes use it before chasing down Strays, to increase physical abilities – and you know the effect it has on those facing exhaustion."

"Very much," he said with a nod. "One of the Rahnzir described me as a Stray, actually."

"Not a surprise. Half the Conclave probably suspect you are a Stray that was able to conceal your lineage."

"And a Stray is what, exactly?"

"Amouni that have strayed from the Path of Purity, and consort with the Common Peoples. Some actually become feral, attacking any and all whom approach. Occasionally, they are used by the Malecaphera."

"Hmmm."

A door closed behind them and Rikeva approached, carrying a small pouch across her shoulder she'd fashioned from the other half of the blanket. "Are we in new danger?" she asked after noting their expressions.

The Guardian mentioned the possible threat at the Phoenix. "We should probably leave as soon as possible."

"One question, before we do," Never said. "Two, in fact."

"I will do my best to answer."

"Is the Great Phoenix in a dormant state?"

"No," she replied. "We aren't fully informed of the cycle, but you were right to assume the Great Phoenix could be met. Again, all the more reason the Conclave might have someone waiting when we reach Her."

"Are there any we can trust among the Conclave? You mentioned calling in favours, didn't you? My memory is a little hazy."

She hesitated. "I no longer believe that I can."

"What of others, like Supreme Jeymiyu?" Rikeva asked. "Was he part of Esuta's trap?"

"I am not certain one way or another," Min replied. "Should we encounter him, I would advise not to trust Jeymiyu, either."

"Leaving only you?"

"Perhaps."

"If we succeed at the Great Phoenix, we might not need anyone else to get home," Never said.

"I hope it so."

"And what of you?" Rikeva asked. "Once we're gone, will you be safe?"

"Yes, but I would keep it secret for now. Perhaps even after you have escaped, for I cannot risk anyone discovering what I plan." She paused. "Not because I do not trust you both. But if captured again, there are ways for the Conclave to take your memories without having to sift through blood in the hope that they would become clear in time. You would not survive such a process, and I fear the Conclave would absolutely stoop to such forbidden acts."

"We won't begrudge you that secret," Never said. "Cheerful as the possibility of forbidden acts may be."

"I appreciate that."

"There is actually one piece of Esuta's plan that I'm yet to understand," Never said after a moment. "Was Rahnzir Sarion meant to capture and return us to the Conclave?

She couldn't have known that we would kill him down there."

"No, but I believe she would have been pleased. Rahnzir Sarion, through his master, Conclave Heracoje, was a very vocal opponent of her plans to subdue a certain people in the far west. Sarion would have wanted you for his plans for defiance."

He frowned at the revelation. "I doubt we'd have done anything different if given the chance, but I don't like having played into her hands."

"Escaping is not to her liking, if that helps," the Guardian said.

"A little."

"Then we should depart, since it's not a short flight. But if you believe the risk is worthwhile, there is a *forasa* close to the Phoenix that we might use."

Perhaps not. "We should fly," Never said, and Rikeva nodded her agreement.

"Then we're best to avoid cities and towns," Min said. "We will have to find food along the way, if you don't mind hunting. Though I must admit, I am not skilled."

Never let his wings free. "You can leave that to us."

# Chapter 30.

No Amouni darted forth on bright wings from the mountainous surrounds to ambush them as they neared their destination. Sunlight struck stone in the Great Phoenix's cavern below, the hushed place appearing empty of threats.

There were no attendants in the cavern either, and Never spied no gardens or benches as he'd half-expected. Instead, just a winding path of stone that led to the enormous, building-sized egg.

And a sense that something powerful waited.

Which was absolutely the case. He descended, setting Rikeva down and landing as Min joined them. After a search for hidden Amouni, unlikely as it now seemed, he stopped before the egg. "I hope I can open this... or at least be heard."

"There's no-one to ask." Rikeva was still looking around. "Don't the Kiymako worship the Great Phoenix?"

"Few are permitted to visit this place," Min said.

"Wish me luck then." He placed a hand against the stone.

No warm glow spread; it was not like when Ayuni woke the bird.

Never called the Holy Fire. Not a blazing inferno, just enough to hopefully be noticed. "Divine One, can you hear me?"

Now warmth spread swiftly across the surface, and the egg split open to reveal a chamber empty of seating. But the familiar nest of black marble waited therein – gleaming detail everywhere; be it bark or twigs, or the mud and dried grass at the base, where several strands hung half-free, as if only recently set in place.

The Great Phoenix roared into light as he approached.

Wingtips reached the smooth walls, the mighty beak looming forth, blazing eyes revealing both power and curiosity.

*You are not of my people, yet you carry a part of my body yet to be born.* Her voice rang out. *Give me your name and purpose, stranger, and let both be pleasing to me, should you wish to live.*

"My name is Never, Divine One. Forgive me for disrupting your rest, but we seek your help to return to a time yet to come. My companions are Rikeva and Min; Min is a Guardian who has agreed to assist Rikeva and I."

*I recognise the Amouni before me, but you and Rikeva are less familiar. Both of the peoples and yet not. You, especially, are not so simple. The contradictions speak of truth or a powerful deceit.*

"I am happy to share my memories, if that is possible? We are not here to deceive, only to find a way home."

*You wish to leave these lands?*

"Yes."

The Great Phoenix seemed to sigh, a flicking of flame from the beak. *You are troubling.*

He waited and beside him, tension seemed to grow from both Rikeva and Min. And why not? The Great Phoenix seemed equally likely to destroy as aid them.

*Not only do I wish to remain free of your memories, but I would find much relief if I could no longer sense the contradictions within you at all.* The Great Phoenix leant over the nest – a gentle movement. *The mere fact that you carry two of my feathers is proof enough that somewhere, sometime, you were trusted. What do you believe I can offer?*

"I hope an answer," Never said, and shared the confrontation with Oleksan, once again focusing on the Eye of Hours. "We don't actually know what happened, or whether we *can* return. Is it possible?"

*Hmmm. That is not for me to say. Even speaking from the ashes of every yesterday, I cannot see every tomorrow.*

"Then, do you know of someone who might be able to help them, Great Phoenix?" Min asked.

*I have not said I have no suggestions of my own.*

"Forgive my offence."

*Merely curb your impatience and hear me. There is something I have been struggling to recognise, something I assumed was a new Amouni aberration. And in a sense, it obviously is. But now that I have met you, Never, the connection is clear. It is linked to you.*

"Another threat?" he asked.

*Not to you or Rikeva. Search the bottom of the lakes where you first appeared, for a hunk of quartz. There is nothing else I can fathom that is connected to your home, nothing else that could possibly enable a return. Even that, I hardly share with certainty.*

A piece of the Eye of Hours? It was something to

seek – a ray of hope, at last! And somehow, it seemed more than probable that the piece she sensed had contained Cog. Never thanked her. "We are in your debt, Divine One."

*Perhaps a debt has already been paid, considering your feathers.* The Great Phoenix flickered and then vanished, only a sharp scent of searing stone left behind.

Never caught Rikeva's smile, but the Guardian seemed less pleased. "Is something wrong?"

"I cannot be sure. After your appearance, we didn't find any unfamiliar quartz when we searched the lakes ourselves." She shook her head. "But I don't think the Phoenix would be mistaken."

"Then let's find out," Rikeva said.

"Of course. We'll have to be even more careful, however. The nearest *forasa* that would be safe is in the mountains above the Temple, which carries its own risk."

"Meaning?"

"Obviously, *forasa* at the Temple and those nearby are all controlled or guarded. We would arrive, and then immediately be captured or discovered. We'd have no chance to search the lake."

"But are you saying the Folhan Ranges pose a larger threat?"

"Not larger. But even old, inconvenient *forasa* are still watched if they lie near a place of note. If we want to remain unseen, it will be difficult."

"Can you create a *forasa* and set it elsewhere on the branches?" Never asked.

"No. In all my experiments, I've only been able to create a temporary symbol for use to reach an existing one."

"Why don't you try, Never?" Rikeva asked. "Your blood is

different. Maybe that will be enough."

It was absolutely worth an attempt. "Where would I place it?"

Min hesitated. "I don't believe I can explain the process to you with language."

"Can you show me?"

The Guardian looked away. "In theory."

Rikeva stepped closer, her voice gentle. "What are you worried about?"

Never understood before she spoke – in the Amber Isle, the ritualistic image of two Amouni, blood spinning between them like dark twine, came to mind. She didn't wish to share his blood. He raised a hand. "Min, it's fine. We aren't going to judge you."

Her shoulders slumped. "Forgive me."

"What does she mean?" Rikeva asked.

Never reminded her of the process to share memories, and comprehension dawned before he'd finished his explanation. Rika placed an arm around the Guardian's shoulders. "Never is right. You don't have to show him. We can use the existing *forasa* you mentioned, we just need to find a way to remain unseen."

The woman lifted her head with a faint smile. "You are both too kind. I am putting you at risk with my weakness."

"You've saved us twice, already," Never said with a smile. "Let's find something to eat, and then we can make a plan."

# Chapter 31.

After another small meal, taken within the cavern but not inside the egg itself, Min described the level of Amouni scrutiny that could be expected when dealing with the little-used *forasa*.

"We are better to wait for nightfall. Guides in attendance will become aware of us when we land, but they don't immediately share our passage with the sentinels. The sentinels will need to either ask or catch sight of us themselves. Which they may well do from their vantage-points," she said. "I'm not familiar with this particular *forasa* – that would be one of my superiors in the Temple."

"How many sentinels are we likely to face?" Never asked, just as Rikeva questioned the location of the watchers.

"Knowing the less-than-diligent Conclave member with jurisdiction over our land, he will have instructed the Temple to post only one watcher. Sentinels tend to be newly-appointed Ascended, and are positioned in a tower that offers a view of cleared land around the symbol."

Never exhaled. The level of exposure seemed to be quite high. Could the sentinel be killed or at least incapacitated before alerting the Temple? There had to be a better way to reach the lake. The lake… Perhaps there was, after all. "What if we find a river? I assume all Guides operate by the same principles, meaning we'd only be discovered if our pursuers ask them directly."

Min straightened with a smile. "You know, I didn't even think of the River-Guides. Being so accustomed to the *forasa*, we rarely consider the old ways."

"Then we need a map," he said.

She nodded. "But remember, your assumption is only true if you keep your blood to yourself. Let me operate any panels that might need to be touched, since that's the only reason we noticed you to begin with."

He nodded.

"Southern Marlosi. There are rivers there that span from Disan and beyond the Holach Forest," Rikeva said. "Is that the case now?"

Min closed her eyes. "I think I know to what you refer, north of the Upper Lake. Yes, there are several *forasa* far enough from the Temples. We should be able to use them, if you're ready."

"We are," Never said.

The Guardian set to work drawing a new, temporary *forasa*. Once completed, she led them through the light and onto a knoll overlooking another abandoned place – this time, a small keep that sat upon a golden plain.

Min pointed to the crumbling stone. "Trade routes shifted, leaving behind such a ruin. There will be inhabited villages to the south, but that is still where we should fly in order to meet the river. Any who see us will be none the wiser."

Rikeva sighed.

"Isn't this good news?" Never asked.

"Yes, but it's one of those times that I wish I had wings. It's not all that comfortable, being carried by my forearms, you know."

"It is not far," Min said.

"I could always carry you as we did near the bottom of the chasm," Never added. Then he raised an eyebrow as something came to mind – something he probably should have realised sooner. "Or, if you like, we could find a Preparation Chamber and awaken your wings."

She opened her mouth to respond… but did not, obviously at a loss for words. Her gaze had not left him either, and when she slowly lifted an arm it was to reach for her shoulder.

"You cannot promise that, Never," Min said with a frown. "Even if, as I assume, she has taken Ascended Blood."

"I have," Rikeva said softly.

"It was a solution we came up with to help her keep down the food here," Never added. "Do you mean that it's less likely for Quisoan-born?"

"Quisoan?"

"Nomadic tribes travelling Marlosi."

"Ah, the *oreyjilar* – or the 'Wanderers', if I were to translate from the old tongue," Min explained. "In short, it would not be less likely for her to awaken a pair of wings. Only less likely to *survive* the awakening. It is not a risk I would advise you take. Some of the more… perverse amongst my people conducted trials. The rate of survival was extremely low."

"That settles it, then," he said as he looked to Rikeva.

"Want me to carry you to the river?"

"That will have to do," she said. "And no more surprises, Never."

"I promise."

"Let me lead." The Guardian released her own wings, which still had a pink tint. She leapt into the air, stirring grass seeds with her wingbeats.

Never took his usual running leap to catch Rikeva, and once they'd gained enough height, able to glide after Min, he helped Rikeva up so that she could cling to him; a rather awkward series of movements that made it hard to keep his balance, especially while moving forward – a different challenge to when he'd simply been able to lock his wings and drift down in the chasm.

He laughed.

Rikeva settled with a frown. "What's funny?"

"If anyone below had seen us, that would have made for a ridiculous sight."

Her expression eased. "I suppose so. This is definitely better, but I'm still hoping for a short flight."

"Let me pick up some speed then."

And thankfully, it was not such a distance to the river's edge, where Guardian Min had already landed. Never was slower to join the Amouni, giving Rikeva time to hop free first. The river was swift and dark, rushing over a mix of pebbles and sand, based on what was visible of the banks.

"Once we reach the lake, how do we search it?" Never asked. "Are we going to need a Guide to help?"

"And how will we use the quartz if we find it?" Rikeva asked.

Ecanseja's memories offered varying detail when it

came to the Eye of Hours – in part due to his deep distrust about the process, but one thing remained clear above all: blood was key, as with so many Amouni artefacts and rituals. "I have an idea of how I might be able to… restore the quartz, *if* that's what we need to do when we find it. But I can't solve the problem of it being under the lake."

"We may be able to use the Guides," Min said. "I doubt there is another way, considering the depth of the Trivium Lakes."

"So, they could find the quartz?"

"Yes. As you know, travelling via river is not quite the same as swimming."

"I do."

"Well, there is a risk but I could have the Guide stop near the quartz, then return us *and* the quartz to an isolated part of the shore."

"What risk?"

"Doing so will weaken the Guide, possibly enough to destroy it. At that point, every Amouni currently in the Temple, Ascended and Greater, would know exactly where to search."

"Could I work on the quartz in a vestibule?"

"So long as you didn't touch the panel."

"Then I think I have a plan. I just need to know, how *you* plan to escape the vestibule. Another *forasa*?"

"Yes." Min smiled. "I don't think any could catch me, even if they follow. I'm a lot faster than I used to be."

"Your wings."

"Yes. Things changed after being possessed by the *semir-ko*."

Welcome news, and no surprise, really. He nodded. "Then I think it's time for Rikeva and I to go home."

# Chapter 32.

The dark river with its streaks of coloured light soon began to change, as Min instructed their snake-headed Guide to stop. It seemed they'd reached the lake already as shadows pressed in, broken only by tiny points of light that were entirely stationary.

"Take us to the quartz beneath the lake," the Guardian instructed.

*Yes, Master.* Already, its head was flickering.

But the pin-prick lights blinked, and then an enormous hunk of purple quartz appeared between them. Or perhaps they had moved and been arranged around *it*. Whatever the case, it worked.

The quartz was clearly left over from the Eye of Hours; Cog's face and torso unchanged from when Never had last seen the man's features upon its surface.

A reminder of his great sacrifice.

Had something of Cog somehow kept the quartz hidden from the Amouni?

"This is worse than I expected." Min was already facing

the Guide. "I'm estimating, but I suspect this Guide will be able to take us to either the vestibule or the shore. After that, it will have been broken beyond repair. It won't be able to move us again, and once it collapses soon after, the investigation will begin."

Never tensed. "Then what choices do we have?"

"Fleeing will be easier from the shore. Alternatively, the vestibule will keep us out of sight from more conventional patrols. I can thwart those who will seek us down here for a time, but not indefinitely. Nor can we stay suspended in this spot much longer."

"Can we call a second Guide?" he asked. "Or a Prime Guide? Wouldn't they be stronger?"

She frowned. "I'm not sure what you mean."

Had they not been created yet? "No matter. Any second Guide then."

"I could, but that would trigger a similar alarm to the destruction of the first."

Rikeva took his arm. "Never, what's your plan? Before we decide."

"Quickly, if you can," Min added.

"While Min works on a *forasa*, I'm going to feed as much of my blood into the quartz as possible. Once this piece of the Eye is reawakened, we're going to touch it again. Exactly the way we found ourselves here, is the way we'll return."

She frowned. "Is that… How do you know it will work?"

"A mixture of what we saw when Cog interfered with Oleksan's plan, Ecanseja's memories of the way blood was used in the construction of the original, and my own instinct," he said with a grin. It was as much an expression of bravado as any true confidence, but despite his doubts, the half dozen ways it could all go wrong, something about his plan seemed *right*. "Anything you want to add?"

"You know better than me. I trust you."

"Good," the Guardian interjected, her gaze still upon the Guide, which was for the moment, still in one piece. "You must choose."

"The vestibule," Never said. "We need privacy."

She gave the command and the darkness was replaced by a tiled chamber, its white and red colours tinted somewhat by the purple quartz.

He called the crimson-fire to his fists as Min knelt to work on a *forasa*. "Tell me if the Guide fails," she said.

"We will," Rikeva replied.

Never sent twin flames into the quartz, though for the most part, he was feeding it blood. The quartz darkened immediately, and a little steam rose. He eased off, decreasing the ratio of flame.

Blood was more important. It was his blood that would save them.

Memories from thousands of lives flowed through him. From his parents back however far their lines stretched, to everything gathered during his years of seeking, whether with Snow or in the years after, to the Blood of the Guardians and every trace of the people he'd met; places he'd visited, the air he'd breathed, the faces of his friends – their smiles; the colour of their eyes, their dreams: every detail that lived within him.

And all of it supported by the feathers given to him by Ayuni, the Great Phoenix.

A history so vast therein, that if a future had to be rebuilt for he and Rika to live within, surely the Eye of the Hours had all it could ever need. And if, as a smaller hunk of quartz, it instead only needed clear pictures of a place to cast only the two of them back toward, then he'd given all it would need.

All that remained was for Rika to carry him to the quartz once he collapsed.

*If* the shard could hold itself together long enough.

Faint cracking sounds rose, but he couldn't stop. The quartz needed more blood; it needed nearly every drop if there was a chance of success.

"Isn't that enough?" Rikeva asked.

"I have to be sure," he said, and it was already difficult to speak between breaths. "Once I fall, you have to carry me there. We'll touch it together."

"I will."

Blood was still pouring forth. More than ever before? It couldn't have been. Not compared to the Stair of Winds. But he had to feed the quartz at least that much. Too little, and he'd fail – and who knew what that would mean? An insufficiently nourished piece of the Eye of Hours could do anything.

Or nothing.

"The Guide has failed," Min said, her voice tight. "We won't be alone for long, but I'll do my best to give you more time."

Never couldn't tear his gaze from the quartz, blinking against a wave of fatigue. It wasn't enough! A little more…

A new figure appeared, looming behind the quartz.

Conclave Esuta.

# Chapter 33.

She was alone and her drapery had obviously been arranged in haste – gold lace missing as her head swivelled.

*Oh, I suspected you would return here, but for what new treachery?*

Never cut the flow of bloody fire. It had to be enough; for if he didn't hold something back now, he wouldn't be able to kill Esuta. "Die," he rasped at her, his voice weak. He called the Holy Fire…

…and nothing happened.

He was empty.

Empty of blood, empty of fire – altogether empty now, but wholly a fool. Of course there was nothing left! Never fell to one knee, teeth clenched as he struggled to stay upright. Min caught him, her own fire blazing.

Rikeva leapt forward, swinging her staff.

Esuta caught the blow on a raised arm. The weapon shattered. Her free hand shot forth and she caught Rikeva by the throat, lifting her up over the quartz. *Whatever you are planning, this abomination must be broken.*

He could not stop Esuta.

Yet somehow, time had ground down to a halt.

The betrayer was mere paces away, yet she might have been back in the Temple for all he could do to reach her. Even Min was blocked – she couldn't send her own fire forth without striking Rikeva.

Never growled.

He was not finished – not by far. Even on the brink of collapse there was still a chance if he was willing to take the gamble of his life...

Nothing would stop him doing so.

"Rika!" Never roared her name. "Pacela's Spire!"

Esuta was already swinging her arm down; Rikeva's cry of rage cut short when she struck and shattered the makeshift Eye of Hours.

It vanished, taking Rikeva too.

Tiny, tinkling sounds filled the vestibule in the silence that followed, little pieces of dark quartz all that remained. There was no way to know if it had been enough, if Rika was safe where she belonged. If anything had changed, at all, anywhere.

No way to follow her with what was left in the vestibule either.

But there was time to take his revenge.

Never let his stakolin side free, even as Esuta glided forward. The woman brushed off Min's blue fire, her drapery suffering not even a singe.

He leapt to meet her with a snarl.

One of her hands reached for him but he swatted it aside – blue skin concealing muscles and bones that bulged as if fighting to break free. He swung again, the second blow hammering down onto her head.

Something snapped, just as the bite of steel cut into his side.

Only, it was no deep wound.

The pain was nothing. Never swung again.

His fist smashed deep into Esuta's body – stopping any further attacks, stopping any further *movement* as he kicked her down. He continued to rain blows upon her prone form. Again and again. Sweat soon dripped from his face.

When he could no longer lift his arms above his head in order to swing down with more force, he began to stomp on her.

Blood was already soaking through the fabric.

New vitality surged through his limbs, merely at the sight – he bent to tear through the drapery with clawed hands.

And froze.

Blood pumped from Esuta's broken neck, but her face flickered… at once a typical Amouni face, and also something more withered, and aged. Both visages seemed to coexist. Her arms were similar… along with her six legs. Six legs?

Legs that protruded from a loose robe of silver.

"Never?"

He turned. Guardian Min stood nearby.

"Yes?" He still wasn't able to speak easily. Even as she drew near, he had to lower himself to the tiles. His skin was changing, his body weakening. Returning to its natural state – thankfully.

"You know their secret now," she said. "Somehow, the Fountain transforms them into something part Guide and part Amouni, if you could call it that. She wouldn't tell me how, before I left."

Never blinked. The Guardian had said something important, but he could not be sure what, for his mind was full of one thought only – getting her promise. But Min's voice had seemed to grow awfully soft, and light in the room was dimming as he lay back. Even his breathing was shallow – he had to tell her, had to explain his plan.

Had to find a way back to Rika…

Never reached for Min but found only air. Had she already used her *forasa* to escape? "Min… promise me."

"I will do what I can." She wasn't gone; she was kneeling beside him.

"If you have… any more favours to call in…"

She sighed. "Perhaps one. If no-one else finds us now."

"Take me to the Infirmary… in Hasollea. Secretly."

"Hasollea? You could recover somewhere closer."

"No. Place me inside… Silver Skin. Promise me, Min. It needs to be hidden… in Pacela's Spire."

"Never, such a place doesn't exist."

He finally caught her hand. "It will. Marlosi capital."

"But there's a cost, you might not –"

"Please."

She squeezed his hand. "I will draw a new *forasa*."

It seemed she kept speaking, but he heard no more as darkness swooped in to cover him at last.

# Epilogue

Summer

Rikeva stared down at the city of Isacina from her saddle. Sunlight gleamed upon grey and white stone and glass alike, with the great dome of the palace among the most boisterous. Or gaudy. Even Pacela's Spire seemed determined to pummel the people below, with its grand spiral construction and pale wings so large…

Would he really be there?

His voice echoed in her head, long weeks later; a shout of desperation. Luckily, his three words reached her before Esuta destroyed the quartz. Damn fool that he was, Never seemed to have a plan.

She nudged her horse down toward the city. "And now I'm finally here."

After splashing into the cold lake, after climbing free to find the Temple Trivium empty, and finding no sign of Ivadr there or anywhere else, Rikeva started north. She spent her time trying to decide what Never had meant. It consumed her in a way that cut into relief at a safe return.

At the fact that nothing had changed for the worse. Home was still home.

No-one lingered near the Temple, and evidence of Oleksan's decay had not just up and vanished from the lands, but at least those she passed on the road, those she purchased a horse from with her Amouni coins, they were all regular Marlosi people whose memories matched her own.

Finally, no hateful, small-minded Amouni flew overhead.

Their tedious gaze gone forever now.

If she was being honest, bearing their disdain each day had been beyond tiresome. The urge to lash out was a constant companion… how many times had her knuckles whitened on her staff?

Killing Sarion had been a welcome release, in some ways.

It was hard to admit how much their sneers had bothered her. Father would have been disappointed. And he would have been right. Who cared what long-dead monsters thought? "My worth has nothing to do with them," she'd told herself as she rode.

And when the capital finally came into view, her supplies running low but her impatience riding high, Rikeva could have leapt down and sprinted the final distance. A strangely satisfying mix of belligerence and hope had her leaning over the saddle, murmuring encouragement to her mount.

Inside the city, she forced herself to keep the people before her in mind, despite their sometimes meandering pace. Forced herself to give way to wagons and Imperial

Soldiers whenever needed, until finally she reached the Spire.

The courtyard was full of stalls where the faithful worked in their pale yellow robes, voices full of cheer.

Rikeva dismounted, giving her mount a pat before handing the horse off to a stable-hand and approaching the doors where silver figures of Pacela waited. More silver. After so long surrounded by so much of it, mostly wrapped around insufferable Amouni, not having to see the colour again wouldn't have been such a bad fate.

A young woman greeted her with a smile. "Welcome."

"Can I speak with the High Priestess? I am Rikeva, she will know me."

Her smile widened. "You're responsible for the cure!"

"Not wholly."

"Please wait inside," the woman replied, her smile only widening. "I will send a message, of course. I'm sure the High Priestess will see you at once."

Rikeva thanked her, following through an arch to the waiting room. There, she took one of the bench seats that faced Pacela's statue in the wheat field, the same one she'd sat before with Never not so long ago.

It felt much longer.

While Rikeva waited, she went over the conclusion she'd arrived at not long after buying her horse.

Based on what she and Never learnt at the Infirmary, there was no other possibility.

He was here… providing his gamble worked.

In time, footsteps echoed along the floor, approaching swiftly. Rikeva stood, only to find the High Priestess herself jogging toward her, braids swinging. The tattoos on Jardila's bare arms brought Min to mind. Had the Guardian survived whatever chaos followed after the second Eye of Hours was destroyed?

Had Never? He liked to play the fool, but underneath, he always had a solution.

"Rikeva, I cannot believe my eyes." Jardila offered a quick embrace. "We thought you and Never were lost! Is he coming? Let me arrange for refreshments."

Rikeva smiled but caught the High Priestess by the hand. "That is why I am here. I need your help."

"You saved us, not only at the Temples, but with your arch-blossoms – anything I can offer, of course. Has something gone amiss?"

"It's Never. You have to take me to the Silver Man."

"But –"

"I'll tell you on the way." She did her best to explain everything to the High Priestess as they ascended the Spire. It was a long tale, but when they finally reached the chamber where the Silver Man waited, Rikeva dashed to it – pressing her hands against the smooth surface.

Something familiar lay within.

Never!

No doubt, no doubt in her mind at all. Just by touching it, she could almost hear the hint of boyish glee in his voice, whenever he said something clever.

Jardila joined her. "How do we wake him? In all the years I have guarded this, before that when I was an acolyte, it has not reacted to anything in any way. Nor for those who led the priesthood before me."

She frowned at her reflection, a little unclear in the silver. "I... don't know."

"There are few we can even seek out for help. Never

held the most knowledge of the Amouni, after all."

Rikeva leant her forehead against the cool surface. "I didn't think this far ahead. It's stupid. I just rode, hoping he was here. And I feel him… but there's nothing I can do."

Or was there? She drew her belt knife, pricked her finger and placed a hand against the silver.

Warmth spread into her palm. Had it worked? Rikeva held her skin against the surface a little longer… then stepped back with a new tension, the tension of hope.

"What is it?" Jardila asked.

"I think…" Rikeva held her breath. Silver began to change as she did. It was slipping away, like rain running down glass to reveal gold beneath. Colours pooled and mixed on the stone floor.

And then, Never was revealed; the makeshift tunic of pale blue that he'd made, his flesh, his face…

He opened his eyes, gave them that Never-grin. "How wonderful to see two of my favourite ladies together."

***

Seated around a small table in Jardila's chambers, Rikeva watched Never as he spoke, content to listen. Most of the weariness he'd been carrying looked to have faded while he slept, and though he explained feeling like no time had passed, in a way, it seemed he *had* woken from a long and restful sleep, rather than the nap he was describing.

A sleep that had even shaved off a few years.

Just a line or two less on his face now; and nothing that spoiled the way he was supposed to look, luckily. A little selfish on her part. His rugged side would vanish whenever he grinned, but she didn't want either to change.

"Were you sure this would work?" Jardila was asking him. "Or that the Eye of Hours would save you?"

"I had a lot of evidence, but it was still a gamble." He shrugged. "Everything was, I suppose."

"And me? Did you know I'd be able to wake you?" Rikeva asked. He'd seemed sure enough while she was struggling with Esuta… Esuta. The creature – in more ways than one, as it turned out.

"To be honest, I didn't get the chance to ask Min about that part. I was just working off what we learnt from the Infirmary, and what I knew of the Silver Man here in the Spire. It *could* have been a Diving Skin."

She sighed. "Then you're too lucky for your own good."

"And yours, right?"

He was grinning again, the fool. "Right."

"Travel throughout time is far beyond me," Jardila said. "It is hard to believe that for centuries, the Silver Man was you, Never. That when you visited it during the invasion, for example, you were somehow also *inside*."

"Well, I don't know if that's how it works. Or whether it was waiting for me all that time. It always felt familiar." He shook his head. "Which doesn't make sense, either. Maybe it was only my potential… I remember feeling that, too, whenever I saw the thing. I didn't have time to ask Min much at all."

"She obviously saved you again," Rikeva said.

Never nodded. "As curious as I am about how she was able to convince generations of Amouni and Marlosi to care for the Silver Man, I mostly hope she was able to save herself."

"I doubt we'll ever be able to find out either." Which didn't seem fair. Min had helped, protected and saved them more than once. Without the Guardian at their side…

An acolyte entered, providing fruit juice before leaving in a rush. Was she flustered to wait upon her leader and the Winged Hero of the War at the same time? Poor girl.

"Perhaps the Guardian made some writings, and they survived somewhere?" Jardila suggested as she took a glass and sipped at the juice. "Did she share nothing else?"

"Actually, one thing," Never replied. "Min mentioned a cost. Something that the healers didn't."

Rikeva leant forward. "Do you feel any different?"

"No. I feel great, actually. It really seems that nothing's changed at all." Never snapped his fingers. "I can still –" His eyes widened.

"What?"

"This isn't…" Never pulled a knife and sliced into his palm, a frown following. "I cannot summon the crimson-fire. *Any* fire."

Rikeva stood.

Blood continued to pool. "And it's not healing right away, like it usually does." His tone had darkened.

"What about your wings?" she asked.

Never slowly lifted his head to meet her gaze. "No."

"What?"

"It's as if they're still here… deep inside. But I can't use them either."

Jardila's voice was hushed. "Are you telling us that all the abilities of your Amouni heritage are gone?"

He lifted his hand, the one he hadn't cut, the one that bore markings of a birch tree. Or *had*. Now, it was just his normal, tanned skin. "I suppose that's the cost she wanted to warn me about."

The High Priestess rose with an apology. "Forgive my lack of manners – I should be organising for your care. I will summon a healer."

"No need to rush," he said, his gaze a little distant. Blood dripped to pool at his feet.

"I will not be gone long." Jardila strode for the door, closing it behind her gently.

Rikeva moved to stand before Never. "We'll get them back. We'll find a way, I promise."

He looked up, and now he was smiling. "That might not be possible."

"What are you saying?"

Never took both her hands in his own. The calluses were rough, and one hand was warm from the blood. "Try not to laugh, but I'm saying that I have everything I need right here. We're together. We survived."

She stopped an admonishment, shaking her head. "You…" She laughed. "You're really not disappointed?"

"I am. But I also meant what I said."

Sincere as he sounded, was he hiding his pain deep down, as he so often had? She squeezed his good hand. "What if I don't want you to give up? I know you, Never. You won't be happy if you can't help people."

"If you really want, we can try. We can wander the lands together, and maybe something will change." He smiled, and leant close to kiss her softly. "But I think I can be happy as we are now, you know."

Rikeva smiled back at him. "I do, too."

# A Note from Ashley

Hello! Thanks for reading Never's 9th adventure – I hope you enjoyed it, and please do let me know if you'd like to read another story following Never and his friends.

I'd like to ask if you could help me out by leaving an honest review of the novel at your place of purchase? Long or short, bad or good, it all helps!

AND if you'd like to sign up to my newsletter (https://ashleycapes.com/newsletter/) you'll be the first to know when the next book is released. You'll also have first access to preview chapters and pre-release editions of the story, in addition to being automatically added into the draw for giveaways.

Ashley

# ACKNOWLEDGMENTS

Above all, thank you to my editor Amanda for saving the day! But also to Lin Hsiang for perhaps my favourite cover art for a Never book, along with Shawn T King for the superb text design once again.

Thank you also to those legends who read the book in its early form and provided such wonderful feedback!

Ashley

# City of Masks Sample

*Book 1 of the Bone Mask Trilogy*

## Chapter 1

The chill of prison bars against his temple did little to ease Notch's headache. Decades of dank didn't help either, nor snoring from another cell, where someone was impersonating a bear. Or dying. In the poor light it was hard to tell.

Notch squinted. Noon sun barely crept through the small, grated windows on his side of the building. Even cells across the way were shadowed. Sunlight, in addition to a piece of bread and some water, were high points, while the straw 'bed' and stale body odour of criminals were typically unpleasant. Worse places than Anaskar City prison existed. At least he hadn't been beaten yet – a twinge in his shoulder reminded him how much some guards enjoyed their work.

His cellmate raised his voice and Notch turned. The man had probably been speaking for some time; his drawn face was expectant. Years of imprisonment had washed out his Anaskari tan.

Notch leaned against the bars. "What is it, Bren?"

"Did you kill her, truly?"

"No."

Bren nodded. "Innocent then." He knelt in the corner, his fine coat of blue long since gone to grime, his face pressed against the stone wall. "Listen to this one." He scratched at an armpit with some vigour. "It's hard to see but I think it says 'death to the Shields of Anaskar' and it's got a signature, but I can't make it out."

Notch grunted. Nothing special for a convicted man to write; since waking on a pile of old blankets that morning and meeting his cellmate, he'd heard a dozen similar sentiments. Through Bren's meandering introduction, Notch had winced, probing his body. Both arms and chest were heavily bruised and his head so fragile he wouldn't be surprised to learn a wagon rolled over it last night. Possibly twice. He wasn't drunk, though the smell of ale was on his breath. One damn drink, that was all.

And there was blood.

His leathers and tunic were splattered a dark red. Not his own blood, the City Vigil told him as much when they hauled him off the street, as if he couldn't figure that much out. But whose? His own memory was unreliable, which made no sense. He hadn't been drunk, truly drunk, since right after the war. When he bore another name. A name he left on some tavern floor, after making a convincing go of drinking the memories away. A good bath did for the sand on his body, but the blood-soaked sand in his mind? No amount of ale had washed that away.

And now the Vigil were telling him he'd been so intoxicated he had to be dragged to the prison?

Unlikely.

"The Shields probably caught him doing something bad, that's why he wrote this," Bren continued, tapping on the wall. His too-bright eyes looked up at Notch.

"I'd say so."

"Like us, Notch. We've done bad things, we have."

"So you keep saying."

Bren laughed, its shrillness cutting through Notch's skull. If it hadn't been unsettling, Notch would have thumped him, but there was something wrong with Bren. Any fool could see that.

"The guards say you've got a few days. That they can't hang you sooner, because there's too many in the queue. Waiting to hang."

"Thanks, Bren."

A moment of quiet fell between them. Distant voices drifted from beyond the prison walls. Notch clenched his jaw. He should have been out there. On his way to another job. The Blue Lady, a fat merchant ship, would have sailed with most of his possessions on board.

His father's sword.

No chance of seeing it again. He wrapped his hands around cold bars and squeezed.

"The guards say it too, the guards say you killed her," Bren said, unperturbed.

"I know."

He crept forward. "So?"

"So I don't remember." He frowned. "But I wouldn't harm a child."

Bren grinned, as if he thought it all a joke, and went back to the wall. A scraping sound followed. "This one says 'down with the Shields' and has no name. I wonder how many people have been here before us, eh Notch?"

"Maybe just you, Bren," he muttered, rubbing at his temples.

Bren prattled on. "I could deal with the Mascare too, you know. They aren't so powerful. It's just their precious bone masks. And their robes. All that crimson. They scare people, the faces. And the eyes too. Did you ever meet any, Notch, before you murdered that girl?"

He ignored the last bit. "I've seen the Mascare plenty of times."

"And were they protecting 'the city, the people and its history' as they love to claim?"

"Each time?"

Bren laughed. "Ever ask them why they won't show their faces?"

"They aren't very talkative, Bren."

Bren stopped scratching and moved to a spot beneath the window, running a set of cracked fingernails over the stone. "This is my favourite. I think it's the oldest one."

The clank of a key in a lock did not deter Bren from his examination, but Notch took hold of the bars again, letting the man's voice recede into the background. At the far end of their row, the guard, a scruffy man who'd made some effort to straighten his blue and silver uniform, led three figures toward the cell.

"Quiet now, Bren," he said as the group approached, their

footfalls echoing. A slender woman – a Lady no doubt – stopped before Notch's cell. She was accompanied by a girl and a stony-faced man with broad shoulders, the orange tunic and gleaming breastplate of a Palace Shield in stark contrast with the prison keeper's appearance. The woman's hair was pulled back from her face, fanning down around her shoulders and covering the collar of an impeccably clean white dress. Bone earrings swung when she turned her head. A sneer that must have been permanent marred her otherwise smooth face.

Notch adjusted his grip on the bars. To come to Anaskar Prison in such clothing – she was either mighty vain or mighty important. Most likely both. Which meant trouble.

The girl stood in similar attire and shared the sneer but had trouble meeting his gaze.

"Here's the mercenary, my lady." The prison guard pointed with his key, making a low bow before scurrying off.

The woman took a single step forward, glaring at him. Her footfall clapped. "Your name?"

He blinked. Her distaste was like a battering ram. "Notch."

The palace guard bristled and she waved a clean hand at him. "Bring the torch, Holindo."

"Yes, my lady." His voice was a rasp.

Behind him, Bren shrunk back into the corner. He did not resume his scraping.

The woman levelled a finger at Notch. "You will address me as 'Lady Cera,' or not at all. Now, do not move."

"Can I ask why, Lady Cera?"

"Because if you do not I will have the Captain here gut

you."

Notch did as he was told. The impulse to wipe her face clean of its expression was strong enough that he had to school his features. Palace folk. Even before he'd taken to the life of a hired sword, they'd looked down their noses at him. 'Mountain Family', they'd say to each other and snigger.

When Captain Holindo returned, the soldier thrust the torch forward, catching Notch's shoulder with his free hand. He narrowed his eyes but said nothing, only adding a crease to his brow. Did Holindo recognise him? Notch couldn't place the man.

"Be still now," the solider said.

The flames singed a little of Notch's hair and he started to sweat. No-one moved or spoke, though the girl he took for Lady Cera's daughter stared wide-eyed at the blood on his clothing.

"Well?" The Lady snapped. "Look. Is it him? Is that the man?"

"I… I think so, mother," said the girl.

Lady Cera and her captain shared a glance before she addressed her daughter again, her tones becoming honeyed. "Dear, are you sure? This is the man they caught by her body, in the street on our way from the harbour –"

"It's hard to tell. I didn't see him that well." She met his gaze. "I suppose it could be this man."

Captain Holindo withdrew the torch. "We have other witnesses, my lady. You've done far more than enough by coming here; it will satisfy the Justice. Furthermore, your own daughter identified the prisoner, that's enough for any man of law." Such a long string of words strained the man's voice, and for the first time Notch noticed a long, faded scar crossing his throat.

She gave a short nod. "Truly. I've had more than enough of this stench in any event. Take my daughter back to the palace."

"Of course, Lady Cera."

He ushered the girl toward the exit. Lady Cera did not follow. "I don't know the whole truth of what happened. But you are a criminal, of that I have no doubt."

"Mercenary, Lady Cera."

"Do you think there's a difference?"

"There can be."

"Well, Notch the Mercenary, I will ensure you hang for this. The girl might have only been a pale-skinned, half-blood brat, but I can ill-afford to replace her."

Notch sneered. "That all she was to you? Something to be replaced?"

She raised her arm but he stepped back.

"Fool." Lady Cera spun and stormed off.

Notch spat. He was already going to hang, what did it matter if some bone-headed noblewoman wanted him dead? Bren shuffled forward and placed a hand on his shoulder. Notch had forgotten him. "She knows what you are. What we are."

"You might be right," Notch said, sitting on the floor and scratching at a new, disturbingly persistent itch in his hair. "But I didn't kill that girl."

# ABOUT ASHLEY

Ashley is a poet, novelist and ex-teacher living in Australia.

Aside from reading and writing, he loves (indoor) volleyball, Studio Ghibli and *Magnum PI*, easily one of the greatest television shows ever made.

www.ingramcontent.com/pod-product-compliance
Lightning Source LLC
Chambersburg PA
CBHW030936210726
48290CB00007B/2208